Late Match

D.W. Brooks

Late Match: This is a work of fiction; therefore, the novel's story and characters are fictitious. Any public agencies, institutions, or historical figures mentioned in the story serve as a backdrop to the characters and their actions, which are wholly imaginary.

Cover design by 100covers.com

Editing by Danyelle Briggs, *In The Write Dyrection LLC*

Formatting by *In The Write Dyrection LLC*

Publisher's Cataloging-in-Publication Data

Names: Brooks, D. W., author.

Title: Late Match / D. W. Brooks.

Description: Houston, TX: Life: The Reboot LLC, 2025.

Identifiers: LCCN: 2025909317 | ISBN: 979-8-9890807-6-2 (paperback) | 979-8-9890807-7-9 (ePUB)

Subjects: LCSH Physicians--Fiction. | African-Americans--Fiction. | Romance fiction. | Lovestories. | BISAC FICTION / African American & Black / Romance | FICTION / African American & Black / Women | FICTION / Romance / African American & Black | FICTION /Romance / Contemporary | FICTION/ Romance / Second Chances

Classification: LCC PS3602 .R66 L38 2024 | DDC 813.6--dc23

Printed in Houston, TX USA.

Contents

As always, to my husband, who always supports me even when it looks like I
might be losing the plot...
To the CWC who always offer support, friendship, ideas, and a virtual shoulder
to cry on during this wild and wonderful journey of writing.
To my editor, we made it! Through weather and illness, we came through.

content warnings

Welcome to my world.

First things first — thank you so much for picking up *Late Match*. This story means a lot to me, and I don't take it lightly that you're choosing to spend time with these characters. I'm so excited (and a little nervous) for you to meet them, root for them, and maybe even yell at them a little along the way.

That said, I want you to go into this book feeling informed and safe. *Late Match* explores themes that may be heavy or triggering for some readers — and while those moments serve the story, they don't need to catch you off guard. I've compiled a full list of content warnings that you can view by scanning the QR code below.

You deserve to read stories in ways that honor your emotional well-being and if you choose to read *Late Match*, I hope it is a story that you will enjoy thoroughly.

1

mackenzie

I should have said no.

The moment we stepped onto campus, I knew it – felt it settle into my chest like wet sand, but I smiled anyway. That's what moms do, right? Fake it until the goodbye hugs hit.

"Mom! Look at those kids racing in the pool!" Alex said, pointing excitedly as if we weren't blocking other people's paths inside. "I can't wait until class! This is so dope!"

Dope was his new favorite word –everything cool, exciting, or vaguely interesting got that label. Not me, though. I was just *Mom*. Or *Momma* if he wanted something. I smiled, but it was a mix of pride and panic. He was growing up fast. He was confident and self-sufficient, and I wasn't ready for any of it. And now I was supposed to leave him here.

For a year. *What the hell was I thinking?*

Alex must have sensed my change in disposition because he hooked his right arm through my left one and squeezed.

"Mom, can you at least *try* to look happy? You look like you're being held hostage." I appreciated the joke. It didn't change much but squeezed his arm back and forced a smile . "Better?"

After glancing at me, he kissed me on the cheek and whispered, "Thanks for trying, Momma."

I gave him a side-eye for the low-key diss. But then his words hit me: I was sucking the fun out of his important day. I took a deep breath. Then another. And another. Nothing was helping.

He was so damn happy to be here and I was the one dragging that down. *So much for being the supportive mom.*

"Don't get me wrong," I said trying to muster some kind of conviction. "I am proud of you! Very proud. You spent the past year doing your homework, your chores, and practicing hard to earn this opportunity. You did what you needed to do to get here."

"Thanks for letting me come, Mom. I know you're nervous, but I'm going to be fine. Trust me," he said, grinning. He looked just like his father when he smiled like that.

That grin used to make me melt. Now it just made the pressures of life worse. His father had already signed off on the trip months ago. Saying no now would have made me the bad guy, and there was no way I was going to be the one to crush his big dream. His *only* dream.

The Olympics.

Watching Phelps on TV with floaties still strapped to his arms, declaring, "I can do that."

I'd smiled at the time. I thought it was a phase, but Alex? He meant it and would never let me forget it. Dr. Stott, his home coach, said he needed more than local pools and weekend races.

"Push him, "He'd told me. "He's got something rare. But it won't show up unless you push."

I didn't want to be that mom. You know, the one who's forcing a dream on a kind who didn't ask for it? There was no point in it. Once Alex had his mind made up, he was going to do whatever he wanted.

So, I pushed.

The UltraElite Swim Academy was one of the top programs in the country. Olympic trial swimmers, actual medalists, all of them trained here. We filled out every form in the application. Sent in the test scores. Submitted videos of his sprints, his endurance trials, the underwater footage, and every angle that Dr. Stott thought they might want.

I even added clips from his local meets just in case they needed proof that my son could show up under pressure.

Then the email came.

He'd been invited to a one-week trial at the Miami campus, and I said yes.

Against every alarm in my head, I said yes.

Dr. Stott had been the one to recommend the Miami campus. Said it had better facilities and more resources. Warmer weather. I pretended that was the reason I was okay with it.

But deep down even I knew that wasn't the reason.

To Alex, I was on "vacation." He wasn't wrong. I rearranged everything in my schedule to be there for him. Parents weren't allowed at every session, but there were windows of time: small breaks and off-campus trips. Enough access to feel fully involved but not nearly enough for me to actually breathe for a second. I told myself I'd hit the beach. Wander a museum. Try a restaurant that didn't have a kid's menu. Maybe even shop a little.

I was supposed to let my guard down.

I hadn't.

Truth was, I hadn't let myself enjoy anything. Not with the thought of leaving my only child at what was basically a swim boarding school in the one place I'd worked to avoid the most.

Because you see, a long time ago, I loved someone who trained at this same Academy.

I mean *really* loved him.

Now, I couldn't walk five feet without running into a memory we'd made or a version of the life we didn't have.

Today was going to be a long day.

And for the first time in forever, it had nothing to do with the amount of times Alex had called my name to show me his backstrokes.

2

evan

I didn't want to come back here.

Not to this building. Not to this campus. Not to the pool where everything almost happened but didn't.

But who was I to tell my twelve year old no?

"Gabe, let's go!" I called toward the bedroom. "We're already ten minutes late, man and you said you didn't want to be."

Trying to get Gabe out of the door on time this morning was proving to be—as always—a Herculean task.

He had his systems, and when they worked, they worked. But when they didn't? We spiraled. Before therapy and meds to help balance his ADHD, mornings like this meant full meltdowns – for all of us. Now, we had structure. Tools. Plans. It was better. Not perfect – but better. And we'd take every win we could get. Especially with everything else we were still learning to co-parent through.

But this trip had knocked him off rhythm. A new hotel. A new schedule. Different wake-up times, and different expectations. Too many variables. Nothing to anchor him. We were operating at a deficit. I knew once we established a routine, he'd be okay. But that wasn't today. Today was about holding it together with duct tape and pep talks.

And praying Grace didn't start micromanaging.

Just as Gabe zipped up his swim bag, there was a knock.

Grace stood in the doorway, looking like she had a spot on the coaching staff. Floral swim set, white bucket hat, flip-flops, and that signature don't-mess-with-me stare.

She slid a tube of sunscreen back into her crossbody. The woman never missed a reapplication window. San Francisco fog or Miami heat — Grace treated UV rays like a sworn enemy.

It was one of the few things we still agreed on.

"Good morning, Evan." She gave me a quick kiss on the cheek as she walked in. "Gabriel, are you ready? We don't want to be late!"

Same message, different parent.

Same eye-roll building in the back of my head. Gabe ran in, hugged her hard, then froze mid-sentence.

"Wait—I need my earbuds!" he said, already pivoting back toward the bedroom.

Grace rolled her eyes at me. "I take it you didn't get him up early enough today."

Nope.

"You could have let him sleep in your room," I said, grabbing my backpack and tossing it onto Gabe's suitcase. "Then you could've had him brushing his teeth at sunrise if you wanted."

Today was registration day. If he nailed it, he could get invited back for the full-year program.

It was his dream — Olympic trials, medals, the whole thing.

I remembered chasing that dream too. Hell, I lived for it once. I started swimming in Mommy and Me classes before I could form full sentences. By middle school, I had a coach. By college, I had routines, scholarships, and Olympic scouts watching my meets. When college ended, I knew I wasn't Olympic material. Not really. With another year or two, maybe I could have made a run at it. But by then, I already had an acceptance into medical school.

I chose the thing that made sense, and most days I didn't regret it.

Notice how I said most?

When Gabe was born, we didn't wait.

He was in Mommy (and Daddy) and Me swim classes before he could walk. He even had the same start as mine. But he had speed I never had. I was a distance swimmer. Gabe? He was built for bursts. Fast-twitch, power, explosion. He was a short-distance specialist — and hungry for it.

"Of course," she said, eyes narrowed . "Gabe just loves staying with me when he could spend the night with you in a cramped hotel room over a perfectly fine suite with his mother. Boys' night, right?"

"Hey, you wanted a quiet tub night," I said, hands up. "I know airports stress you out. I was just doing my part." I glanced over at her. "We watched movies. Ate junk. He was asleep by ten. You enjoy your solo night?"

Grace smiled at me. "Yes, I had a lovely massage at the hotel spa. I also ordered room service—some New York cheesecake—it was simply divine. This is a really nice hotel." Then, she plucked a rumpled shirt off the couch like it offended her. "Can we try not to destroy the room? Or is this a man cave now?"

"This is the man cave," I said, hands sweeping across the chaos like Vanna White. "You have spas. We have sports, snacks, and laundry piles. It's sacred."

I smirked. "Let us live."

Grace threw the shirt at me and started to laugh too.

Gabe ran back in just in time to catch the end of our joke.

"Hey, I need that shirt! I've been looking for it!" He snatched it off my shoulder and dashed back into the bedroom.

Grace sighed. I reached out and gave her shoulder a pat.

These mornings got to her more than they did me. I rolled with chaos. She planned around it. I thought last night's calm would carry over. Clearly, I overestimated us.

Having a quiet night was important for me, too. This place pulled memories out of me like teeth — slow and aching.

Grace and I both agreed Gabe should stay with me. I'd already started scouting options to move my neurosurgery practice down here just in case he'd gotten into the Academy. One less transition if this became long-term. Grace hadn't committed yet. She said it was about her GI practice. But I knew what was really holding her back.

We had work to do. Structures to rebuild. The stakes were higher now and she wasn't about to uproot her life for a maybe. It needed to be definitive before Dr. Grace Robertson would ever make a move so big.

Grace turned away from me and started playing with the handle of Gabe's suitcase. "So... how are you doing? Being back here, I mean." She cocked her head at me. "Tell the truth."

I cleared my throat. I should have known Grace was going to bring that up. "I'm trying not to think about it," I glanced toward the window and back at her. "But yeah.. This is all... different now. Reminds me of my Olympic dreams and the things I didn't chase.... Med school... I paused, shrugging my shoulders. "And her."

Grace didn't even flinch, "Not surprised."
"But that's not why we're here," I said cutting her off before she could even get started."We are here for Gabe. Not me and my mess..." I rubbed the back of my neck. "What is taking him so long?"

I could see Grace watching me. Grace didn't say anything. Just kept watching me.

Like she could still read what I wasn't saying.

"Stop looking at me like that," I muttered. " You're making it worse."

I checked my watch and my chest tightened. "Gabe, let's go!"

A wave of memory crept up before I could block it — her laugh, her name, her face by the edge of the pool.

Not now. Not here.

We needed to leave.

Gabe rushed out of the bathroom, now fully dressed — and back to being in charge.

"Let's go! I don't want to be late!"

He flew past his suitcase like it didn't exist. Grace and I locked eyes.

No words. Just a silent exchange of here we go again.

She grabbed the suitcase, and we followed our son out the door.

3

mackenzie

I should've worn sunglasses.

Not because of the Miami sun – though that was blinding enough – but because everything out here was too bright. Too loud. Too real.

To our left: the Olympic-sized pool, glittering and blue under an aluminum roof. To our right: a running track, then a massive white tent with bold REGISTRATION banner flapping in the wind. The whole place was packed – at least one hundred teenagers and their families, scattered between the pool and the sign-in tent, buzzing with energy as if this was the Olympics already. And just like that, the panic I'd been holding off all morning started to creep back in.

But I kept my face straight. He didn't need my nerves clouding his day. I forced a smile, squared my shoulders, and followed him through the crowd. Someone clipped my foot on the way past. I glanced down at my white high-top Converse — no smudge.

Thank God. Those shoes had survived residency. They weren't going down today.

We were supposed to meet Alex's father here to handle the paperwork.

But punctuality had never been one of David's core values. And as I expected, the texts started flying well after his original arrival time:

David

> Lo siento, guapa. I'm in the parking lot. Where are you? I'm coming to you!

Of course, he was breaking out the Spanish. He only texted like that when he was flirting or about to be late and usually it was both. David's mother was from Valencia, the third largest city in Spain, and between her accent and his years playing pro ball across Europe, he spoke Spanish like a second skin. It had been one of his aces – with women, with the press, with everyone.

And yes, I'll admit it: back then?

It worked on me, too.

Me

We're heading to the registration tent. You'll see me. I'll be the one flipping you off.

David

Querida… don't be mad. I'm almost there. Ten minutes. Te encontraré.

I rolled my eyes. "Te encontraré," my ass.

He wasn't even on the property.

I dropped my phone into my purse and turned to tell Alex his dad was on the way – and blinked.

When had he gotten taller than me?

Somehow, we were eye-level. Again

He'd passed me – officially. I was 5'10" on a bad day. David was 6'6". And Alex? He was already towering at 5'11" and growing like he had something to prove. His feet were too damn big, his shoulders were starting to square out, and the baby face I used to kiss every night now had faint hints of stubble.

He was built for the water. Built for this place.

Just like his father, the realization hitting me harder than I expected.

Alex stood next to me, bouncing slightly on the balls of his feet, scanning the crowd like he'd been doing this his whole life. Confident. Ready. Like he belonged here.

And he did.

I was the one who didn't. Not anymore.

I needed a distraction. Something useful. Productive. Something I could control. So I pulled out my tablet and opened my patient portal, tapping through new messages as if it weren't a form of medical-grade denial. Just two prescription requests – both flagged by my nurse with those little "your call" notes she loves to add when she knows they'll piss me off. I reviewed the first, double-checked the dosage on the second, and approved both with a tight little nod like that solved anything.

And just like that — boom.

The last task was done. No more messages. No more charts.

I was officially on vacation. For the first time in fourteen years.

I'd promised myself – and Alex – that I would try. No calls. No consultations. No answering patient emails from a hotel balcony while pretending it was "self-care." Just one full week off full of sand, sleep, and overpriced cocktails with way too much sugar and not enough rum.

It felt impossible.

The last time I took a real break from work was back in my second year of residency. We took a weekend trip to Vegas after a 28-hour shift, and I was so sleep-deprived I couldn't remember half the weekend.

What I do remember? The tequila. The wedding chapel. The man who made me laugh so hard I forgot my last name – and apparently took his instead.

I still don't know how the marriage was legal. I didn't know his real last name until after the vows were done. Didn't know I was pregnant until six weeks later.

That man? David Witten.

My ex-husband. The same one I was waiting on now. The same one who helped me make this brilliant, lanky, overconfident swimmer standing next to me like he already owned the damn place. And sure, our marriage didn't last. But we got Alex.

And that's more than I ever could've planned for.

A flicker of movement caught my eye. When I looked up from my tablet, Alex was still scanning the crowd—but something had shifted. He wasn't bouncing on the balls of his feet anymore, and his easy grin had disappeared. His jaw was tight. Shoulders tense. And for the first time since we arrived, he pulled out his phone to check the time.

That's when I knew.

He was starting to get irritated.

Alex never got irritated with David. Not really. He'd spent most of his life learning how to manage his father's version of "on time." He knew to expect the extra fifteen minutes, the "I'm almost there" texts that meant nothing. Usually, he let it roll off his back. But not today.

Today, he was trying not to care – and my baby was failing.

I slipped my tablet back into my tote and glanced at the time. Twenty-five minutes late. So much for "ten."

My eyes swept the parking lot again, but I didn't see that obnoxious bright red Jeep David insisted made him "look fun." I almost laughed. That car wasn't fun. It was loud, impulsive, and about as reliable as its driver. Just like everything else David touched.

Alex let out a long breath and shoved his phone into his pocket, eyes still darting through the crowd.

I touched his arm, lightly. "He'll be here soon."

He gave a small nod, not looking at me. Just enough to say he heard me. Not enough to believe it.

That nod cracked something open in me.

I'd spent the last three weeks preparing for this moment, and not a single second of it was spent calming my emotions or thinking about how to say goodbye. No, I prepared the only way I knew how: I threw myself into planning.

Target became my therapy.

I shopped like my sanity depended on it. Linens, towels, shower caddies, drawer organizers. I ordered three different comforters and sent two back because the stitching didn't feel sturdy enough. I color-coordinated his toothbrush holder with his laundry basket. Bought snacks he hadn't liked since middle school, just in case he changed his mind. There was even a dolphin-shaped lamp in one of his bags – a callback to his "marine life" phase from age nine that I clearly wasn't ready to release.

"Mom, it's one week," he kept telling me. "Not forever."

Didn't matter. If I couldn't stop time or slow down his growth or fix the tightness in my chest every time I imagined walking away from him...

Then damn it, I was going to organize the hell out of his room.

Control what you can.

As we continued to wait, a young blonde woman with a tablet approached us with a questioning look on her face. She couldn't have been more than nineteen – maybe twenty – with a perky ponytail, a blinding white UltraElite Academy polo, and that kind of overly bright smile you only develop after years of customer service or competitive cheerleading.

"Are you here to register for the One-Week Swim Blast?" she asked Alex directly, eyes locked on him like I wasn't even standing there.

I arched one brow.

Her name tag read ADDY, and her whole vibe screamed summer intern trying to impress someone. Her tone was light, flirtatious, casual in a way that made my stomach twist. Not because she was doing anything wrong, exactly – but because she was flirting with my son. My thirteen-year-old son, who looked like a full-grown man when you didn't know better, and who absolutely did not need some teenage blonde batting her lashes at him before registration.

Alex, bless him, didn't even clock the shift in her voice. He looked to me first – a small gesture, but one that still knocked the air out of me—and I gave a tiny nod. Go ahead.

"I'm Alexander Stephens Witten," he said, polite and clear. "W-I-T-T-E-N."

Addy typed quickly, her eyes flicking to him and then back to the screen. She swung her ponytail to one side as she worked, almost theatrically. And then – because of course – she giggled. Giggled.

Oh, so she *was* flirting with my thirteen-year-old.

I was seconds away from saying something sharp when her smile suddenly froze. Her eyes narrowed at the tablet screen.

"Um," she said, tone shifting hard. "I'm sorry. I need a parent to complete this. I didn't realize..."

She turned to me then, all business now that she'd apparently scrolled down far enough to see the birthdate.

"Ma'am, what's your name?"

I took my time before answering.

"Dr. Samantha MacKenzie Stephens," I said evenly. "His mother."

I watched her posture straighten as she tapped in the information. Now she was all yes-ma'am and policy and procedure. She asked for Alex's birth date, our address in Nashville, my phone number, and the name of the coach who referred him. I gave her everything quickly, precisely. No extra smiles. No small talk.

Let her learn something today.

When she got to the payment section, her brows pinched again. "It looks like the system still requires Mr. Witten's signature and payment information to complete registration. Is he here?"

"I'm here," came a too-familiar voice from behind us, rich and smooth with just enough dramatic flair to make me roll my eyes before I even turned around.

David Witten jogged up, a little sweaty, all charm and swagger, wearing that grin that used to get him out of trouble and into my bed. He was still in ridiculous shape – light golden-brown skin glistening just enough to let you know he'd parked three rows away on purpose so he could show off the run. He kissed my cheek before I could stop him, murmuring his apologies like they were supposed to mean something now.

I didn't bother responding.

He was lucky I didn't introduce him to Addy and tell her he was the one who needed flirting today.

Alex lit up the moment he saw his father. "Dad!"

They launched into one of those elaborate, over-the-top handshakes that only the two of them knew. Slaps, snaps, spins – it was ridiculous and perfect. I had no idea when they'd created it, but it was theirs. One more thing David managed to get right.

"They're waiting for you to pay," Alex said, grinning. "And Mom is annoyed with you because you're late again."

David laughed as he pulled out his wallet. "That's my boy. Always honest."

He tapped his Black Amex on Addy's tablet with a little flourish, like he was sponsoring the damn camp himself. Leave it to David to make an entrance – even with a payment.

"It took you long enough," I muttered, poking him in the shoulder.

"You know I'm worth the wait," he said with a wink, slipping the card back into his wallet like he hadn't just thrown off my entire morning.

I rolled my eyes but didn't push. That was our rhythm—friendly, casual, cordial, as long as he didn't cross the lines we'd spent years carving into stone.

It hadn't always been that way. In the beginning, it was chaos. Arguments over drop-offs. Late payments. Missed birthdays. And when the divorce finally settled, we realized we had two options: stay enemies or figure it out.

So, we built a system. We set boundaries. No flirting. No fighting. No touching my tongue, my tits, or my tail. His rules, my words.

And somehow, it worked.

We weren't friends. We weren't enemies. We were just parents – raising a kid who deserved the best of both of us, even when we were at our worst.

David glanced over at me and smiled, but this time it was smaller. Realer. The one that said he knew I was holding it together for Alex's sake. I gave him a tiny nod back. Just enough to say I saw it. Not enough to let him in.

"Alright, superstar," David said, clapping a hand on Alex's shoulder. "Let's get you settled."

Alex grinned so wide it nearly cracked his face, and in that moment, I let myself breathe.

Even if I didn't belong here, he did.

And that was enough.

4

mackenzie

Being a pediatrician paid the bills. It even paid for a few indulgences. But this camp? This entire experience? It was well beyond my budget.

Swim Academy fees. Equipment. Travel. Private coaching. When you stacked it all on top of Alex's other needs and school programs, it was a financial mountain I couldn't climb alone.

But David? He had climbing gear.

His mother came from money – the kind that gets passed down in heirlooms and old wine cellars. A Spanish family with land and names you find on plaques in opera houses. His father was just as formidable: a self-made African American executive who turned a mid-size business into a multi-million-dollar legacy. Together, they built a foundation for David that included elite schools, world travel, and every opportunity money could buy.

Sure, he had challenges growing up – being an Afro-Spaniard wasn't easy – but access wasn't one of them.

Then came the basketball career. Overseas leagues. Endorsement deals. A flashy stint in European sports culture that only added more commas to his bank account.

Alex benefited from all of that. Too much, sometimes.

I tried to teach him restraint – tried to instill values that weren't measured in price tags. I reminded him often: Your father's money is not your money.

But David? David was a walking contradiction to every lecture I gave.

Once the receipt flashed across the screen, Addy straightened her posture like she'd just closed a sale.

"Alex, would you like me to take you over to the booth to get your welcome package?" she asked brightly. "There's a couple of t-shirts, a polo-like mine," she twirled dramatically and gave a tiny curtsy, "and other goodies in the bag. I'll bring him right back."

That last part was aimed at us, the parents of a minor, the kind she probably expected to protest. Alex turned to us like she'd just offered him the keys to a car

"Please?" he asked David, not even bothering to ask me.

David nodded. "Sure, son. I need to talk to your mom anyway. We'll be right here."

And just like that, they disappeared into the crowd.

David didn't miss a beat.

"Te ves genial, como siempre," he said, smooth as ever. "Me gusta que ahora uses lentes de contacto. It lets your gorgeous eyes shine."

I shot him a warning look. "You flirting or apologizing?"

"Can't it be both?" he grinned.

And just like that, I was back in Barcelona.

Not Vegas.

Barcelona.

Six months after Alex was born. We were still pretending we could make it work, visiting his parents, playing house overseas like it wasn't all crumbling back home. I remember standing in his mother's kitchen, still exhausted from jet lag and nursing, and David wrapped his arms around me from behind, whispered something in Spanish I barely understood, and made me laugh so hard I dropped the wine bottle I was holding.

I don't even remember what he said. Just the way it made me feel. Like maybe – just maybe – this whole thing could be real. Like we could be real.

"Stop looking at me like that," I muttered, turning back toward the tent. "It doesn't work anymore."

"Didn't say I was trying," he said, but he was smiling like he knew better.

I ignored it.

"How long are you staying in Miami?"

He shrugged. "All week. Figured I'd watch how Alex does, see if this place is really worth leaving him in for months."

I blinked. "You're staying the whole week?"

"Yeah. What? You thought I was just going to drop in, pay the bill, and disappear?"

Yes. That was exactly what I thought. That was what he usually did.

"Well, don't expect me to play tour guide," I said, folding my arms. "I came here for rest. I want at least three beach days, two overpriced dinners, and one museum visit where I don't have to answer anyone's questions."

He put a hand over his heart. "So serious, doctora."

"I'm on my first real vacation in years," I reminded him. "You don't get to derail it."

"Oh, right. You and vacations. One broken engagement and one surprise marriage — you're, what, 0 for 2?"

I narrowed my eyes. "Watch it."

He dragged out the name like it tasted good in his mouth. "Evaaaan."

God, he was so annoying but also... not wrong.

I exhaled sharply. "You said you weren't trying to get on my nerves today."

"Who said I wasn't?"

I turned to scan the crowd for Alex, more to avoid eye contact than anything. "Let's not do this."

"I'm just saying—"

"I know exactly what you're saying, David. And I don't need the reminder."

He didn't flinch. "You still haven't looked him up, have you?"

I didn't answer.

David crossed his arms, suddenly quiet. "You know I was never jealous, right? It wasn't even about him. It was about the way you kept that space in your head carved out for someone who wasn't coming back. A man who ghosted you before ghosting was even a word."

I clenched my jaw. "I'm not doing this here."

"I'm just being honest."

I hated when he peeled me open with the same softness he used to swaddle our infant son. Always so casual, so composed, like the truth wasn't heavy on his tongue.

"You weren't letting me in. Not all the way," he continued. "Not when it counted. And you're still not letting anyone in. Evan's been gone fifteen years, Mac. Whatever happened, whatever he did or didn't say, it's not now. You're still holding your breath, waiting on closure that isn't coming."

I blinked away the sting behind my eyes and turned toward the registration tent. "Maybe I should go find Alex."

David's face softened and he took one step back. "I shouldn't have brought it up. My bad."

I didn't say anything. Just kept my arms folded tight across my chest, like I could keep it all inside if I held on hard enough.

He bumped me gently with his shoulder. "You know I only bug you because I care."

I rolled my eyes. "You bug me because it's fun."

"Both can be true." He paused, studying my face. "You good?"

I nodded, just barely.

He pulled me into a hug before I could protest. "You still look amazing, by the way."

I elbowed him, but I didn't pull away.

We stood there in silence for a moment, watching the crowd buzz around us. I could feel the weight of what he'd said lingering between us, but for once, he didn't push. Just stood beside me, still and steady.

"I'm in therapy, you know," I said after a beat. My voice was quiet. "Been back for a while."

David looked over at me, surprised. But he didn't crack a joke or make it weird. He just nodded. "Good. That's good."

I hesitated, then added, "Maybe... after the summer, after this whole swim academy whirlwind is done... I might look. Just to see. Not to reopen anything. Just to know."

He didn't say anything. He didn't need to.

Because that was enough.

Because he knew me.

And in that moment, I let myself believe – just a little – that maybe letting go wasn't the same as forgetting.

"Now go find our son," I said, clearing my throat and stepping away from his hug. "Before he runs off with the welcome package and gets himself a new family."

David laughed, that big, warm belly laugh that always made people turn and smile. "Yes, ma'am."

And just like that, the moment was over.

But something in me had shifted.

Just a little.

5

evan/mackenzie

We checked Gabe into the Academy first. Got the duffel, the gear, the welcome spiel.

He unzipped the bag right there in the middle of the path like it was Christmas morning. T-shirts, a schedule, a water bottle with the UltraElite logo —it was all standard stuff. But to Gabe, it was gold. Twelve years old and already halfway out of childhood, eyes darting past us to the older swimmers like he was ready to join their ranks. Grace and I tried to walk him through a few reminders—alarms, routines, staying on schedule. I don't think he heard a damn word.

"Look at all the guys here with tattoos, Dad!" Gabe whispered, wide-eyed. "Some of them are almost as cool as yours."

I leaned in. "No tattoo talk in front of your mother. Please."

The Poseidon on my chest wasn't a story she appreciated. Neither did my own mom, for that matter. Gabe had been begging for ink since he was eight. It wasn't happening.

Grace heard anyway. Her eyes narrowed. "You'll be with boys your age. I'm not a swimmer, but I know fast when I see it. You'll be fine."

I nodded. "They'll group you by age, stroke, distance. Don't stress. Just get in there and show them what you've got."

Grace pulled out her phone and snapped a photo of us mid-convo. "The Robertson boys," she said with a little smile.

Gabe was in the middle of a growth spurt—5'8" and gaining on both of us fast. He'd pass her any day now, and I wasn't far behind. Once he reached my 6'2" though, then we'd be having some different conversations.

"You're growing like a weed," she said, peeking at the photo. "And God help you—you're starting to look like your father."

We all laughed. Family joke. Might not be nice, but it worked.

Just then, one of the academy's older swimmers stopped to ask Gabe if he wanted to tour the grounds with some of the other boys. Gabe hesitated, but we nudged him forward.

"Go," I said. "We'll meet you back here in thirty."

He gave us a little nod—half cool guy, half still-my-baby—and took off.

With him out of earshot, Grace and I started walking. Since we were among the first families to register, we had time to see the facility before things got too crowded. I'd been here before when Gabe and I toured different programs around the country. But Grace? This was her first time. So, she had questions.

A lot of them.

"What's the age range?" she asked one of the counselors near the dining hall. "Our son's not the youngest here, is he?"

"Nope," the counselor said. "We've got a couple younger girls, maybe one eleven-year-old boy. Girls mature quicker at this age. They handle the pressure better."

Grace didn't flinch. "And curfew? Supervision? How many counselors per room?"

The poor guy answered every question without blinking. You could tell he was trained for the parental gauntlet.

I stayed quiet. I appreciated the way she handled it—sharp, precise, a little tense. Her questions weren't just for show. She was worried. Watching her move through each space like she was building a mental blueprint of the week made me realize how much of this she was doing on faith.

We left the dorms and kept walking.

"It's a nice facility," she said finally. "He's going to have a good week here. I might still pick up a few things for his room, though. Towels, maybe a blanket. Something personal."

That... surprised me.

I wasn't sure she'd ever really been on board with Gabe doing this, not fully. She wanted to wait another year. Give him more time. But this was the year—academically, athletically. We both knew it. This was the window.

"Thank you for the compliment," I said.

She raised an eyebrow. "Was that a compliment? My bad."

I laughed. Classic Grace. Sharp tongue, soft heart.

One of the reasons I'd fallen for her in the first place.

By the time we circled back to registration, Gabe had already found a new friend — one I didn't know would change everything.

MacKenzie

After David's hug, I felt better. Calmer. Maybe I could actually have a decent time this week.

I checked my watch again. Alex still hadn't returned with his goodie bag. I craned my neck toward the last place we saw him and nudged David. "Do you see him? He should be back by now."

David followed my gaze. "I see him. He's standing over by registration talking to a couple of people. Let him enjoy himself for a few more minutes."

That flicker of calm I'd been holding onto started to fray. "We have to get him into the dorm. I still need to add the towels, blankets, rugs—"

David burst out laughing. "He's thirteen, Mac. Please don't tell me you brought themed gear. What is it? Pound Puppies? Wonder Twins?"

I rolled my eyes, but his grin cracked my frustration. "First of all, it's Paw Patrol, Pound Puppies, or Wonder Pets. Second, The Wonder Twins were a Super Friends cartoon from the eighties. Which, I'll remind you, you definitely watched."

"Oh! Pensé que me sonaba familiar," he said with a smug little smile, still laughing.

I was about to roast him for the accent, but the mood held. We were laughing together again—for once—and it felt good.

Until I felt a hand on my shoulder.

I turned to find Alex standing beside me, beaming, a sleek Nike duffel bag with the UltraElite logo slung over one arm.

"Let's see what's inside!" I said.

David reached out and took the bag, unzipping it as Alex launched into full ramble mode.

"There's some really primo stuff in here," he said. "Oh! And I met a guy over at registration. He's a sprinter. His family's here too, they're on their way over. Maybe we could all go to dinner or something—"

He was talking a mile a minute, the background noise from the crowd washing over half his words, but I could still catch the excitement in his voice. While he talked, David pulled item after item out of the bag, holding each one up for my inspection.

The quality was surprisingly nice. I picked up one of the shirts and held it against myself. "Could I borrow this?"

"Mom, Mom!" Alex tapped my shoulder, urgent now. "They're here."

I turned just as my son said, "This is Gabriel. And his parents, Mr. and Mrs. Robertson."

The whole thing unfolded in slow motion.

David looked up the same moment I did. Smile freezing instantly. Eyes wide and knowing.

And me?

My heart stopped.

6

mackenzie

Evan Robertson, MD, stood in front of me—in the flesh—with his hand extended like this wasn't the most surreal moment of my year.

Fifteen years. Fifteen years since I'd seen my ex-fiancé. Since the night we fell apart. Now here he was, standing in the Miami sun, and suddenly I couldn't breathe.

Just seeing his eyes—the way they studied mine, curious and unbothered—brought it all back. Med school. The chaos. The laughter. The breakdown. The loss. The almosts.

But mostly?

It brought back the day we met.

I'm 100% sure it was the blouse that sealed the deal with Evan.

Specifically, the top button.

We all have that one outfit that makes us feel powerful. Mine was a tailored dark green button-up and a fitted black skirt with a kick pleat. I wore it to my med school interview. I wore it to orientation. That shirt? It was my armor. The first piece of clothing that ever made me feel good about my body—especially my chest. The tailor had cinched it perfectly at the waist, and for once, I felt put-together, not just covered up.

Spoiler: that shirt didn't survive the night.

I was at the welcome reception, trying not to look as anxious as I felt. Two tables: one with envelopes of paperwork, the other with snacks and a bowl of red punch that looked like something out of a lab spill. I'd taken an anxiety med before walking in, just enough to dull the panic and keep me talking. Hopefully.

A few nice students tried to make conversation, but small talk wasn't my thing. I stumbled over every word and eventually gave up, retreating toward the corner with a cup of radioactive punch in one hand and my pride in the other.

That's when he walked in.

He was 6'2", light-brown skin, hazel eyes, a mass of perfect curls, and a smile that practically needed its own zipcode. I locked eyes with him for half a second and felt it in my stomach. Like heat. Like warning.

And then he walked right up to me.

"Hi there. I saw you hiding back here. You guarding the punch? Because, no offense, I don't think anyone's planning a heist."

I laughed. Out loud. Like a real laugh.

He grinned like he'd earned something. "I'm Evan Robertson," he said, pointing to his nametag. "Former competitive swimmer. Now, apparently, a med student. And you?"

"S-Samantha MacKenzie Stephens," I said, mortified. "Everyone calls me Mac."

"MacKenzie," he repeated slowly, like tasting wine. "I like that."

He asked me why I became a doctor. I told him about the promise I'd made to my mom and grandma—how I wanted to be a pediatrician because of my brother's chronic illnesses. It wasn't the whole story, but it was enough.

He told me he wanted to be a neurosurgeon because of his grandfather, who'd had a benign brain tumor. After surgery, his seizures stopped. Evan wanted to give that kind of healing to someone else.

He leaned in when I spoke. I found myself wanting to keep talking just to stay close to him. It wasn't like me. But it felt right.

"It's loud in here," he said eventually. "Wanna go outside?"

I followed him. And I didn't look back.

Even though everything around me moved—the swimmers, the traffic, the splash of the pool—time had stopped. He was here. Evan. After all this time.

And he wasn't alone.

He had a wife.

He had a son.

That last one shouldn't have shocked me as much as it did. I had a son. I picked this academy because of him. Because of what he'd said years ago when he was a med student. Because I trusted his opinion. Because, even after everything... some part of me still clung to the idea of Evan Robertson.

I'd never looked him up. Never called when his father passed. Never reached out, even when I wanted to. And now I was standing here, staring at him like I was twenty-four again and hadn't cried myself to sleep every night for a month after our breakup.

He looked... perfect.

Trim hair, tighter curls. Still swimmer-cut, with arms that probably swam laps before breakfast. T-shirt sleeves stretched over biceps like he'd never left the pool. And his hands... those hands.

I should not be thinking about those hands.

I tried to blank my face, but a little voice inside me whispered: You care.

You care what he thinks. You care how you look. And yeah... you'd let him ruin you again if he asked.

I sucked in a breath and tried to shake it off.

I was a grown-ass woman. A pediatrician. A single mom. I wasn't about to be undone by a flash of hazel eyes and a memory of the best sex of my life.

But damn if it wasn't tempting.

What the hell was I supposed to do now?

7

evan

I 'd already stuck out my hand to shake Alex's mom's when she looked up—

And froze.

One look at her face and I was gone. Not here, not in the Florida sun.

I was back in med school.

I walked into the med school welcome reception thinking two things:

One: I was ready.

Two: I needed to keep my shit together.

No distractions. No drama. No emotional baggage. I had a plan—become a neurosurgeon, keep my reputation spotless, and make it through four years without becoming a headline.

And then I saw her.

She was tall, Black, and beautiful, standing by the refreshment table with a cup of suspicious red liquid and a look on her face that said please do not talk to me. Naturally, I made a beeline.

I didn't know what I was doing. I just knew I had to talk to her.

She looked a little like she was trying to disappear into the plastic plants behind her. Maybe it was nerves. Maybe it was the world's worst fruit punch. Either way, I grabbed a cup, made a lame joke about her guarding it, and waited to see what would happen.

She laughed. A real one. That was it for me.

Mac.

That was what she called herself. Samantha MacKenzie Stephens. She was quick with a smile and slower with her words, but once she relaxed a little, I could tell she was sharp. She made a joke about her name like she was hosting The Price is Right, and I couldn't stop staring at her wrists—slender, delicate. The kind of wrists you kiss without meaning to.

She told me she wanted to be a pediatrician because of her brother's medical history. I told her I wanted to be a neurosurgeon because of my grandfather's tumor. I was trying not to come on too strong, but it was getting harder with every passing second.

When the crowd got louder, I asked if she wanted to step outside.

The moment we hit the patio, I spotted the Olympic-sized pool and stopped walking like I'd just found religion. Mac laughed at my face and said something teasing—right before someone bumped into her.

She stumbled. I caught her.

And then we were falling.

Straight into the damn pool.

The next few seconds moved in fast-forward. I hit the surface, spun around—no Mac. Panic set in. I dove down and found her at the bottom. Limp. Eyes closed.

Shit.

I got her to the surface and shouted for help. Arms pulled her out of the water. I followed, dropped to my knees, and started mouth-to-mouth. Nothing.

I leaned down, desperate, and whispered in her ear: "Don't go. I just found you."

Still nothing. Then she coughed. Sat up. Spit out what had to be a gallon of chlorinated water.

And just like that, I was gone. Fully, permanently gone.

Seeing her again short-circuited every rational part of my brain.

Mac.

She was standing in front of me with her son—our sons were friends?—and I couldn't even pretend to be casual. My whole body locked up. My hand was still halfway out like I was a wax figure at Madame Tussauds.

MacKenzie. After fifteen years.

She looked... unfairly good. Like the universe was mocking me.

That green maxi dress clung in all the right places. Her skin glowed in the sun. The white Chucks? Still somehow her. And those braids, long and loose down her back—

God. She'd always worn her hair natural, but something about this version of her felt more grounded. Older. More powerful. More Mac.

I couldn't stop staring.

Then I saw him. The man standing next to her. Tall. Athletic. Familiar, in the way that annoyed me instantly.

Was that her partner? Her husband?

My chest tightened.

I wanted to say something smooth. Funny. Casual. Something that showed I wasn't still dreaming about her, still haunted by the day she walked out of my condo after our final fight. But all I managed was... nothing.

I just stood there like an idiot. Mouth open. Heart racing. Brain short-circuiting.

This wasn't how I imagined seeing her again.

Then again... I never imagined it would hurt this much.

8

grace

That shift in Evan's energy. Like something had cracked the air around him.

We were standing there, all smiles and easy banter, when suddenly… he went still. His shoulders didn't rise with his next breath. His eyes locked on something over my shoulder. And for just a split second, he looked like he'd forgotten how to be a person.

Then I turned.

And there she was.

Samantha Stephens, MD.

Even before she introduced herself, I knew. Of course, I knew. You don't live with someone like Evan—love someone like Evan—and not notice the moments when they're somewhere else. Or with someone else in their head.

He never said her name often. But when he did, it was like everything else in the room dulled. And when he didn't say her name—when he skirted around it, when he paused midsentence and changed topics—those were the moments that told me everything.

Back when we were friends, he spoke about her with this complicated tenderness. But when we got married, that tenderness turned into something heavier. Like regret. Or unfinished business. I told myself he was just mourning the "what if." That it would fade.

But even after Gabe was born—even after everything we built—there were days I could still feel the ghost of her name hanging between us.

It's not like I ever blamed her. She didn't do anything wrong. She wasn't texting him. Wasn't reaching out. As far as I knew, she was living her life. She was just... present. Unshakably so. Some women linger like perfume. She was one of them.

And now? She wasn't a memory anymore. She was real and right in front of us. And still gorgeous, in that put-together-but-effortless kind of way that makes you question if your edges are laid properly.

I caught David glancing toward me at the same moment I glanced at him.

He looked like he'd seen a ghost, too. Or maybe a damn soap opera. His eyebrows shot up, like, You catching this?

I gave the smallest nod.

Without saying a word, we both just turned toward the boys and started walking, like we'd been given a mission we didn't ask for but were suddenly very invested in. A few steps later, David pulled out his phone and said, "What's your number? Just in case we lose each other in the chaos."

I handed him mine without a second thought. I blame motherly instincts.

Grace

You ever just know when it's not about you?

David

Yeah. Felt it today. Right in the damn chest.

Grace

I knew Evan still thought about her. I just didn't real-ize how much.

David

Well I never thought I'd have to stand in the same room as him but alas here we are.

David

So what now?

Grace

We give them and maybe… if they can find their way back to each other, at least somebody gets the happy ending.

David

It's not the one I wanted. But it's one I can live with. If she's happy… maybe I'll finally stop wondering if I was ever enough.

Grace

You were. So was I. We just weren't it. Not for them.

David

So we smile. And keep the boys distracted. And maybe pray they don't waste this second chance.

Grace

I'll raise a plastic concession cup to that.

I slipped my phone back into my pocket just as we reached the front of the line.

"What do you two want?" I asked the boys, glancing between them.

David raised a brow. "You just gonna let them pick anything? You do know they're thirteen, right?" He turned toward the boys, hands on his hips like a weary sitcom dad. "Alright, you two — pick a drink. Something without enough sugar to send you to the ER."

Both boys groaned in unison.

"Dad," Alex said, dragging the word out. "Mom's not here. You don't have to do all that."

David pointed over his shoulder, toward the cluster of trees where we left their parents. "And yet, she's always watching. I value my life, son. I'm not trying to get cussed out before noon."

I couldn't help it — a real laugh slipped out. Gabe and Alex rolled their eyes but eventually settled on fruit-flavored water. David ordered two more bottles, this time without asking.

"For them?" I asked, already knowing the answer.

He shrugged. "Just covering my bases. I figure they'll need something cold while they melt in all that tension."

I glanced over my shoulder toward the clearing. Neither of them had moved.

"If they're even talking," I muttered.

David passed me one of the waters and gave a quiet, almost resigned nod. "Yeah. But even if they aren't, they won't be the same after this."

I let out a slow breath. "It's gonna take more than one conversation."

"Good thing we've got a week," he said.

We started walking back, drinks in hand, the air a little heavier than before.

And still — somehow — hopeful.

9

evan

After our pushy exes disappeared with the boys, I glanced over at Mac. She was staring at her Converse like they held the answers to the universe. Some things never changed. Whenever she got nervous, her eyes always found the floor.

But the silence between us? It was thick. Uncomfortable. We hadn't said a word to each other since she introduced herself to Gabe—and that barely counted.

I cleared my throat. "Hi, Mac. Small world, huh?"

Her name came out easy. Familiar. Like it still belonged to me in some way.

She let out a breath of a laugh and shook her head, her gaze still glued to the ground. "I never imagined running into you like this. And definitely not like this. With... kids."

I watched her, trying to gauge the space between us. "I'm surprised Alex swims," I said, hoping the shift to something neutral might settle us. "Given how much you hated the water."

Her head snapped up.

"You didn't think I'd keep swimming?" she said, defensive now. "You taught me. I didn't stop. Not really. Okay, sure, not every day during residency, but once that was over? I got back in the water. And I put Alex in it as soon as I could. It became... important."

The way she said that — quiet, insistent — hit harder than I expected.

I opened my mouth before I could stop myself. "But you could let *me* go?"

She blinked. Once. Then twice.

Shit. That came out harsher than I meant.

"I'm sorry," I added quickly. "I shouldn't have—"

"No, you really shouldn't have," she cut in, her voice tight. "This isn't the time or the place."

I nodded. But my heart was pounding. "I didn't even get to say goodbye," I said, a little softer now. "You FedExed the ring back, Mac."

Her arms folded across her chest. "You think I wanted to do that?"

I took a step forward. "I think you didn't give me the chance to understand."

"And I think you refused to see me!" she shot back, louder now. "What I needed, what I was going through—none of that mattered to you back then!"

A few heads turned.

Mac swore under her breath and turned away, trying to regain control. Her shoulders rose and fell like she was holding something back.

Just then, the cavalry arrived. Grace and David returned, boys in tow, drinks in hand. David passed Mac and me each a bottle without saying a word.

Mac took it, quietly, eyes still red-rimmed. She tried to angle herself away from Alex, but he'd already clocked her face.

"Mom? You good?" he asked, stepping closer.

He turned his eyes on me, hard and cold. The kind of look that said *you hurt my mom and I'll end you* — and damn if I didn't deserve it.

Mac recovered quickly, hugging Alex and brushing him off. "I'm fine, baby. Just got a little emotional thinking about old memories. It's not a big deal." She sniffed and gave him a smile that didn't quite reach her eyes.

Alex didn't buy it.

David moved in to flank his son, keeping the energy low. I nodded in silent thanks.

Grace stepped in like the pro she was. "Speaking of old memories, Mac, I need you to see the monstrosity I've planned for Gabe's dorm. He's going to hate it. It's going to be beautiful."

Mac exhaled a laugh. "Don't tempt me. I have a whole duffel bag of 'just in case' decorations."

The boys groaned on cue.

"Moooom."

"You two should be grateful," Grace said, turning to them. "This is love. Love in the form of throw pillows and color-coordinated comforters."

"Love or prison?" Gabe muttered.

Alex leaned toward him. "Yeah, I'm about to have a bed skirt and I don't even think it's legal."

Mac raised an eyebrow. "Keep it up. I'll hang fairy lights."

David tried to stifle a laugh. "They're definitely going to regret this conversation."

I cleared my throat, finally jumping in. "Alright. Let's make a plan before they end up grounded before day one."

David nodded. "Big Pink. It's in South Beach—family friendly, good food, strong drinks."

Gabe lit up. "Is it near the water? Like actual beach beach?"

Alex perked up. "Can we go? I've never really had a beach day. Not in Nashville."

Mac hesitated. Her eyes flicked toward me, unsure.

And then — she nodded. "Okay. Vacation mode. Let's go."

My heart did something dangerous.

The door hadn't just cracked open.

It was ajar.

10

mackenzie/evan

Fourth year of med school is when things start to feel real. You're done with the grind of third-year rotations, and now it's time to decide where you'll actually *become* a doctor. That means diving headfirst into the black hole of residency applications — transcripts, essays, letters of recommendation, test scores, interviews. It's a full-time job on top of the one you already have just staying afloat.

Evan and I knew what we were getting into. The couple's match process was tough —two people trying to line up their futures on paper and hope an algorithm thought you were worth keeping together. We applied to programs in six cities. San Diego, San Francisco, Nashville, Atlanta, Chicago, and Birmingham. We both ranked UCSF first.

Evan's match mattered more. Neurosurgery was one of the hardest specialties to break into. Pediatrics wasn't easy, but it wasn't neurosurg. I told myself I'd follow him anywhere.

I even started to believe it could all work out.

That December, he proposed. Around the same pool where we first met. He got down on one knee and gave me a two-carat princess-cut platinum ring. It was beautiful. We were planning a wedding on Catalina Island — just after our intern year.

For once, I let myself dream. Really dream. Not the half-hearted kind where I was waiting for the other shoe to drop.

And then... Match Day.

Evan's name was called first. "University of California, San Francisco."

He whooped. I cried. The good kind.

And then it was my turn.

I opened the envelope expecting the same four words.

But it said Vanderbilt University. Nashville.

I stared at the page. Evan stared at me. The cheering stopped. The future cracked right down the middle.

We tried to stay calm. Evan hugged me, whispered that we'd figure it out. But my hands were shaking. I couldn't even hear Adrienne's voice as she pulled me into a hug. I was stuck in the thought: *Of course this happened. Of course the universe wants me to be alone.*

There was no pediatric slot for me in San Francisco. Not for this year, anyway.

We made calls, sent emails, begged. UCSF promised to take me the next year. So that meant twelve months apart.

Evan was optimistic. But me?

I already felt the loss blooming in my chest.

Evan

When I pulled out the slip of paper from my envelope and saw *University of California, San Francisco*, I felt like everything we worked for had been worth it. Mac was next to me, her hand gripping mine. I remember the way her nails dug into my palm—a mix of nerves and hope.

We kissed. The whole room erupted in cheers. Our classmates had watched us go from strangers to inseparable. This felt like the storybook ending.

Then Mac opened her envelope.

She didn't say a word at first.

Just stared.

I saw the way her eyebrows pulled together. The flicker of confusion. Then she slowly turned the paper toward me. *Vanderbilt University. Pediatrics.* My stomach dropped.

We both stood there. Frozen.

Someone nearby whispered, "Oh, no…"

The cheers around us faded to silence, and I realized how quiet the room had gotten. No one knew what to say. A few people offered weak smiles, pats on the back. Adrienne, one of the girls from Mac's study group, made her way over and hugged Mac before I could react. She was crying now — quiet at first, then not so much.

I wrapped my arms around her and tried to ground us both. "It's okay. We'll figure it out. It's just a mistake in timing. That's all."

But I could feel it — the walls going up. She wasn't hearing me. Not really.

We left the conference room, and I got her into my car. She didn't speak on the ride home. I kept glancing over, watching her try to keep it together. Her lip was trembling the entire time. The kind of tremble that comes when you're trying not to scream in public.

That night, I sat on the floor with her in my arms. She curled into me, wearing one of my old swim meet shirts. She kept apologizing like she'd failed us.

"We were so close," she whispered. "We were so close."

"I know," I said. I didn't know what else to say.

Around 3 a.m., we started listing every hospital we could think of in the Bay Area. UCSF. Stanford. Kaiser. County programs. Mac jotted everything down on a legal pad, her handwriting getting sloppier as the hours passed.

We made calls. Sent emails. Got silence or soft rejections in return.

By the end of the week, UCSF offered her a deferred spot. A guarantee for the next year.

"We can do this," I told her. "It's one year."

She gave me a small nod. But I could already see the shift.

She wasn't breaking up with me — not yet — but something was slipping. Something small but steady. Like a knot loosening one thread at a time.

She stopped talking about wedding plans. Started working longer shifts. Said "I'm tired" a lot. And eventually, *I don't know if I can keep doing this.*

I should've fought harder. Or maybe I fought the wrong way — kept trying to solve it like a problem, when what she needed was for me to just *see* her.

She was grieving. And I missed it.

She FedExed the ring back exactly twelve months later.

And I didn't even get to say goodbye.

11

evan/mackenzie

Although there were four vehicles between the adults, getting all six of us to the restaurant somehow turned into a sitcom pilot.

Once the boys found out David had rented a Porsche, it sparked an immediate battle royale for the front seat. It nearly turned into an impromptu wrestling match right there in the parking lot. Grace, clearly not in the mood for bloodshed, jumped in.

"Gabe, maybe you can ride with Mr. David on the *way back*," she said, in her best let's-not-lose-our-minds voice. "There'll be plenty of time to ride in the Porsche. Right now, let's not make a scene."

She glanced over at David to make sure he was cool with it. He gave her a laid-back nod.

"Although I have a Camaro, which is *just as cool*," she mumbled under her breath.

"It's really not," David replied, eyes twinkling as he turned to the boys. "But let's not burst your mom's bubble."

Grace narrowed her eyes, then swatted at his offered handshake with a laugh.

"I'll take you out in the Porsche one day—change your mind," he told her smoothly, before turning his attention to Mac and me. We were standing off to the side, keeping our distance like two magnets flipped the wrong way.

"Maybe you two should ride together," he added. "No need for all the cars. The boys want the fun rides. Grab one of the Tahoes and meet us there."

How subtle.

I squinted at him. He smiled like butter wouldn't melt in his mouth. If he hadn't married the love of my life, we probably would've been great friends.

"Grace, could you hand me my keys?" I asked, more reluctantly than I intended. I'd given them to her earlier when we first arrived.

Grace passed them to Mac instead of me. Mac didn't meet my eyes as she handed them over—and when our fingers brushed, the spark was instant. Physical. Undeniable.

She jerked back like she'd been shocked. The keys slipped. Clattered against the pavement.

"Sorry. I thought you had them," she mumbled, stepping away.

I bent down, picked them up. "It's fine."

From the corner of my eye, I saw Grace and David exchange a look.

"Let's get these boys some food," Grace said. "They're lookin' like limp biscuits."

David burst out laughing. "*Qué horrible!*"

She shrugged. "I said what I said."

They weren't wrong. Gabe and Alex had gone from jumping around like excited puppies to slumped teens camped out on the Porsche, flipping through their camp gear like it might hold the secrets of the universe.

"Sitting's never a good sign," Grace added, still speaking directly to David. That was new. She wasn't usually this... dialed in. I had a hunch it had something to do with Mac. And not in the "we're flirting" kind of way. This felt more like co-conspirators trying to steer a ship through a hurricane.

David clapped his hands. "Let's go, boys. Big Pink's calling."

As if on cue, Gabe and Alex perked up. Grace and David got them into the cars like professional child wranglers and drove off without a backward glance—leaving Mac and me alone in the parking lot.

We stood there for a minute or two, just watching the taillights disappear. Neither of us moved.

"You coming?" I asked.

She kept staring down the street, like maybe they'd make a U-turn and save her from whatever this was about to become.

I exhaled hard and stayed where I was. "You want to drive your rental?" I offered. "Lead the way?"

"I—" she paused, rifling through her purse. "I left my keys in Alex's duffel."

Of course she did.

I walked over to my rental, climbed up onto the running board, and left the door open. "We're really gonna do this here? In a parking lot?"

Her mouth tightened. I heard her mutter "Fuck" under her breath. That was still her go-to when the universe didn't follow her script.

I watched her debate it silently. She looked the same but not—more confident in her body, softer in places but sharper in others. She wasn't wearing glasses anymore. LASIK? Contacts? Didn't matter. The woman was still breathtaking. And that dress—God help me.

But we had to eat, and this moment was about survival. Not seduction.

"If you don't come on, everyone else will be eating while we're still standing here making this harder than it needs to be," I said.

A dad walking by with his kid paused and pointed toward me. "Are you going somewhere good? I'll ride with you if she doesn't. I love free food."

Everyone nearby laughed. Even Mac cracked a reluctant smile. Without another word, she walked over and got in the passenger seat.

"Fine. I'll guide you."

She buckled her seatbelt like it was a seat on a rocket to hell.

I slid behind the wheel. The radio was still on. A Gap Band song played low through the speakers—*Outstanding*. The same song I sang to her, off-key, at my sister's wedding.

I didn't say a word. Neither did she.

She gave me clipped directions and kept her eyes forward. That was the entire ride.

We pulled up twenty minutes later. Grace had just finished giving the hostess our name, and we were seated within minutes.

If there was one upside to our stubborn silence, it was skipping the line.

MacKenzie

I didn't want to ride with him because I didn't trust myself not to say something that would set the whole damn day on fire.

Or worse—kiss him.

Seeing Evan again was like being drop-kicked into a memory. He looked incredible. Older, yes—but still carrying that easy confidence that always made me feel like I was trying to catch up. And now, I wasn't sure if I wanted to slap him, hug him, or crawl into his lap and cry.

And of course, our exes were playing matchmaker. How the hell did *they* manage to become friends that fast?

I'd been blindsided. I wasn't ready for this. Not for real conversations, not for apologies. I needed space. Time. A plan.

By the time I got into the car, I'd at least reined in the worst of my reactions. I gave him directions. That was it.

When he started the engine, *Outstanding* floated through the speakers.

I remembered. His sister's wedding. The slow dance. Him singing the lyrics in my ear like a love song written just for us.

But I didn't say anything.

I didn't even look his way.

If we were going to survive this week, we couldn't afford to peel back the past too soon. Not yet.

Maybe not ever.

12

mackenzie/evan

Our year of separation after med school was a disaster from start to finish.

When Evan and I started dating, I became someone I hadn't been in a long time, maybe ever. Steady. Grounded. Proud of myself. I had worked through the worst of my anxiety. I was doing the self-work. I'd gotten through school. And by the time we walked that stage, I'd come far enough that my doctor took me off my meds entirely. I honestly thought I could handle long-distance.

Then residency hit.

Our hours got brutal. We were both working around the clock, and I started feeling like I was dating his voicemail. Half the time, I'd call just to hear his voice say "leave a message." By the end of September, I'd spoken to the nurses in San Francisco more than I'd spoken to him. And one of them in particular — Christine — was entirely too familiar.

She wasn't direct. Women like her never are. Just... comments. A string of carefully placed lines meant to sound innocent enough that I'd look crazy calling them out:

"Oh, I told him you were on the phone, but he'd already left with a few of us for lunch."

"I didn't know he had a girlfriend!"

"You must be really understanding. I'd never let someone like him go."

"Oops, that came out wrong."

That woman weaponized passive aggression like it was her job. And maybe it was. Maybe she had one goal and I just happened to be in the way. Either way, it worked. Because it didn't take long for me to start unraveling.

Every time I brought her up to Evan, he brushed it off. Said she was harmless. Said I was overthinking it. That there was nothing going on. But he never actually addressed it. Never told her to back off. Never said to anyone at work that I was his fiancée. And that silence started to eat at me.

It wasn't just her. It was the way he wouldn't protect us. Not from her. Not from anything. And the more I tried to hold it together, the worse it got. I started thinking it was my fault like maybe this was just what long-distance couples go through. I told myself it would pass. That once I moved to San Francisco in June, it would all fall into place.

I was wrong.

When I finally got a few days off in January, I flew out there hoping we'd have a chance to reset. Evan had been teasing some kind of surprise —something that might ease the distance between us. I told myself it was a sign. That maybe, despite everything, we were still okay. He left a key for me at the front desk. I let myself into the condo, walked straight into his closet, and pulled one of his old T-shirts over my head like muscle memory. It still smelled like him. Like warmth. Like safety. Like everything I'd been holding my breath for. I curled up in his bed and waited.

He got home around seven. We ordered Chinese. I tried to catch up. Talk. But Evan had other plans. He walked into the bedroom, peeled off his scrubs, and smiled at me like we hadn't just gone half a year without touching each other.

And for a second, I forgot everything I came to say.

We didn't talk that night. Barely ate. Barely slept. We stayed tangled up in each other, like maybe if we kept our bodies close enough, the rest of the problems would fade.

They didn't.

The next day felt almost normal — made breakfast, ran to the store, worked out together. There were a few moments where I actually let myself believe it was going to be okay. That we'd just needed time. That the hard part was already behind us.

That night, he said we were going to a get-together for his department. One of his attendings was hosting, and Evan seemed excited to bring me. I still had questions. Still needed to know what the hell was going on with his coworkers. With Christine.

While we were getting ready, I brought her up again.

"Is Christine going to be there?" I asked through the shower door.

He paused. "What?"

"Christine," I repeated. "Is she coming?"

He poked his head out of the glass like I'd asked if the Pope was invited. "Why are you asking about her?"

"I've talked to her more than I've talked to you," I said calmly. "Figured I should know who she is."

He rolled his eyes. Said she was just a nurse. That I'd like Mitchell better — he was funny, from Georgia.

I didn't push. I didn't need to. I already had my answer.

By the time I finished getting dressed and put on my heels, I had made peace with one thing: if this night went left, I was done pretending not to notice.

And sure enough, it went left immediately.

The moment we stepped into that party, I could feel it. Most of the people there didn't even know Evan was engaged. Not because he'd kept it private. Because he hadn't said it at all. The introductions were polite. The compliments were warm. But there was a certain tone, like I was a surprise. Like they weren't expecting someone like me.

Then I met Christine.

She was shorter than I expected. Pretty in a unsettling way. Perky. Friendly. Fake.

When Evan turned to talk to someone else, she stepped right into my space with a smile and said, "You should see him in the OR. He's really good with his hands."

I smiled back. "That's great. He's a talented guy."

She leaned in. "I just didn't realize he was engaged. He doesn't act like it."

I didn't take the bait. I didn't cause a scene. But I saw exactly what she was doing.

Evan came back. I let him think everything was fine. But the mood had shifted.

Christine spent the rest of the party haunting us. Always close. Always watching. Always conveniently next to Evan in every group conversation.

And then, just like that — she vanished.

I wish that had been the end of it.

But we hadn't even hit the worst part yet.

Evan

We got home late. The car ride back from the party was mostly quiet, except for the occasional deep sigh from Mac that said more than any words could. She didn't even take off her heels before heading inside — just beelined toward the elevator like the night hadn't ended, like she was still trying to hold it together until she had a door to slam behind her.

The moment we stepped into my condo, I knew something was off.

It wasn't the lights. Those were still off like I'd left them. It wasn't the scent of takeout lingering from the night before.

It was Mac.

She didn't say a word, just walked straight down the hall like she owned the place. Like she had every right to.

And then I heard her yell.

"The fuck?!"

My heart dropped. I sprinted after her, already knowing it wasn't good.

When I hit the doorway to the bedroom, she was standing still, staring at the bed like it had betrayed her.

And there she was. Christine.

Wearing one of my dress shirts like it belonged to her.

I froze, bile rising in my throat. "The fuck?!" I shouted, echoing Mac. "Christine—what the hell are you doing in here? How the fuck did you even get in?"

She was sprawled out on my bed wearing nothing but one of my shirts. And it wasn't even buttoned.

She sat up fast, startled. I guess she hadn't expected me home so early. Definitely hadn't expected Mac. She clutched the shirt closed, trying to salvage her pride, and said the dumbest thing she possibly could've:

"Sorry. I didn't know you were going to be here, Dr. Stephens."

Mac's laugh was quiet. Cold. "Maybe if she knew you were engaged, she wouldn't be here now."

Christine opened her mouth to say something else, but Mac had already clocked the pile of clothes on the floor. She picked them up, turned toward the window, and tossed everything — bra, panties, jeans, heels — straight out of the fifth-floor window like she was taking out the trash.

"Leave the shirt on your way out," she said, not even looking at Christine anymore.

Christine gasped. "What am I supposed to wear to get my clothes?"

Mac reached down, grabbed one of my dirty scrub tops off the floor, and held it out. "This'll cover your ass. Barely."

Christine looked at me, waiting for... I don't even know. Sympathy? Rescue?

I didn't say a word. I couldn't. I knew Mac was right. And I knew I had fucked up.

Christine took the shirt, ducked into the bathroom, and when she came out, Mac was waiting again.

"Keys," she said.

Christine froze. "What?"

"The key you used to get in. Give it back."

I stood there, jaw clenched, while Mac kept going. "I don't know how you got it — probably stole it off his lanyard one day and made a copy. Doesn't matter. Leave it. And get out."

Christine hesitated. One last desperate glance in my direction. I held out my hand. She dropped the key into my palm like it burned her. Then she turned, walked out the door in my oversized scrub shirt, and didn't look back. I locked the door and stood there for a second, trying to breathe. Trying to process the nuclear-level fallout I'd just caused. When I finally walked into the kitchen, Mac was leaning against the fridge, drinking a beer. Which was how I knew she was done. She hated beer.

"I'm sorry," I said. "I'm so fucking sorry. I doubted you. I didn't listen. You know I always try to see the best in people—"

She stepped forward. "That's not a strength if it means stepping over the person who loves you to do it."

"Mac, I didn't invite her here. I didn't even know—"

"She shouldn't have felt comfortable showing up like that in the first place. She shouldn't think I'm invisible."

"She doesn't."

"Evan," she snapped. "You introduced me to your boss and your coworkers like I was just some girl you were seeing. Nobody there knew you were engaged. Nobody knew who I was."

I looked down. Couldn't argue.

"So when I told you she was answering your phone or making slick comments, did you ever tell her to stop? Did you tell HR?"

I shook my head. "No. I didn't want to make it a thing."

"Too late," she said. "It already is."

I tried again. "Nothing ever happened."

"I believe you," she said. "But that's not the issue."

She stepped away and turned her back. "Are you going to report her now?"

I hesitated. "That could ruin her career."

"And?"

"She didn't touch me."

"She broke into your place and climbed into your bed. What if I hadn't been here? What would've happened then?"

I didn't have an answer.

Mac set the beer down. "Still protecting your residency. Still thinking about your future. Not about us. Not about what it costs me every time you let someone else take my place in your life."

"Don't say that. You're everything to me."

She blinked, hard. "Then why am I the one who's been hurting this whole time?"

I could feel it—the moment when something shifted. When something between us cracked wide open.

She kept talking, but now her voice had that tremor. The one that meant she was fighting to stay calm.

"I wanted to break up before graduation," she said. "I knew I couldn't do long-distance. But I loved you, and I didn't want to give up on us. And now? Now I'm barely hanging on. I've been spiraling, Evan. You don't see it because you're not there."

"We can fix this."

"I don't know if we can."

She looked up at me, and I saw it—all of it. The grief. The exhaustion. The quiet decision already forming behind her eyes.

"I need more," she said. "More than phone tag and ghost messages from jealous nurses. I need to feel like I matter to you in a way that's not just theoretical."

"I do love you. So much. That's why—" I stopped myself. "That's what the surprise was. I didn't want to bring it up like this, but Vanderbilt still wants me. I talked to them. I can transfer next year. Come back to Nashville. Be with you."

She froze.

Then: "You can't do that."

"What?"

"I can't let you move your entire career for me. I can't be the reason you walk away from this opportunity."

"It's not walking away. It's choosing us."

"It's sacrificing something you've wanted your whole life. And the second you get frustrated or unhappy, I'll wonder if it's my fault."

I stared at her. "Mac..."

She shook her head. "I've carried other people's sacrifices for years. I can't carry yours too."

I didn't know what to say. I'd never seen her look so... resolute.

"Let's just talk in the morning," I said. "Please. Let me hold you tonight."

She let me.

And later that night, we made love like we were trying to tattoo the memory into our skin. Like if we just stayed tangled up long enough, we wouldn't have to let go.

But in the morning, she was already packed.

I sat up, heart thudding. "You're leaving?"

She didn't answer at first. Just zipped her suitcase.

Then she walked over, kissed me soft and slow, and said, "I love you. But I need space. And you need to stay here."

"But—"

"We're not ready. Not for a transfer. Not for forever. Maybe not even for right now."

I couldn't breathe.

She crossed the room, sat on the couch, and pulled out her phone to order a cab.

"If we can just get through this time of separation." I tried to hug her but she shook her head and took a step back.

"If," she said quietly, like the word itself broke her heart. "That word's doing a lot of heavy lifting in your sentence."

And just like that, she was gone.

We didn't talk again for fifteen years.

13

evan

"No blood," David muttered as Mac and I returned to the table at Big Pink. Both he and Grace gave us that parental once-over—like they were checking for bruises or broken pride.

They don't know how close it came to getting ugly.

"Ha ha," I said flatly, spinning slowly so they could see me intact. I went to pull out Mac's chair in some half-assed attempt at chivalry, but she sat too fast. If I'd moved it, her ass would've hit the floor.

Chivalry took a blow to the nuts.

Luckily, no one noticed.

Before I could regroup, Gabe was already bouncing in his seat, waving the menu. "Dad! They have a burger with waffles as the bun. What are you gonna get?"

Grace stepped in. "Sweetheart, your father just sat down. Let the man breathe."

So began the chaos. Orders flew around the table. Pub-style apps hit the center—potato skins, spinach dip, something deep-fried that none of us could name but we ate anyway. While the adults picked, the boys had David telling stories about playing basketball overseas. Some of it wasn't even PG. Grace jumped in with track stories from her college days, and before long, it felt almost normal.

Almost.

Except Mac and I kept sneaking glances at each other like this was high school. If I caught her looking, she turned away. If she caught me, I pretended to be interested in the salt shaker. It was subtle enough for the kids to miss—but not the adults.

Grace kicked me under the table. Once. Twice. By the third time, Alex clocked it.

"Dr. Grace, why are you kicking Dr. Evan?"

Grace, completely unfazed, replied, "Because he's being an idiot. It's a form of communication."

I shot her a glare. Everyone laughed. Except Mac. And me.

Dessert made things worse.

Fried Oreos hit the table, and both boys lost their minds. They were halfway to sugar comas and full-blown slap-happy by the second bite.

"Momma," Alex moaned, chocolate stuck to his chin, "why have you been hiding this from me?"

Mac reached over to wipe his face. He tried to dodge her, grinning like a gremlin. "I'm going to eat one every day while we're here. Maybe forever!"

Grace arched an eyebrow. "Given how you boys brush your teeth? Let's not." She stabbed one of Gabe's Oreos with her fork to taste for herself.

Chaos erupted. Gabe launched a counterattack for her pie. Alex dove into Gabe's plate. David, cool as ever, slid Alex's dessert out of reach like a blackjack dealer clearing the table.

Just as the madness peaked, Mac stood.

"I need some air."

She reached into her purse to leave cash for her half-eaten plate. David stopped her with a hand wave. "I've got it."

I watched her walk out of the restaurant, the air shifting in her absence.

David leaned back in his chair and stretched. "I'd go after her if I were you. I'm staying here to digest."

Grace nodded, already brushing crumbs off her dress. "Might be your only window."

They weren't wrong. If we were going to get through this week without imploding, someone had to break the silence. Might as well be me. She stood out front, facing the line of obnoxiously pink Volkswagen Beetles the restaurant used as mascots. I stayed a few feet behind, hands in my pockets.

"You okay?" I asked.

She didn't turn around, just kept staring at the cars.

"I can't believe people actually drive these things."

Mac tilted her head, just enough for me to catch the curve of a smile. "My mom would've loved them. Hot pink was her favorite color."

"I remember."

Silence. But not the tense kind. Just... quiet.

She shifted first. "Things going well in San Francisco?"

I nodded. "They are. I'm on track to lead my department one day. But if Gabe gets into the year-round program here... I'm moving to Miami."

She looked over, brows raised.

"I need to be close. He doesn't have a big extended family, not really. And if he's training seriously for the Olympics, he'll need all the support he can get even if he pretends he doesn't."

She folded her arms across her chest. "I've thought about moving too. For Alex. But he doesn't want to say it out loud. He doesn't want to make it harder."

Another pause.

Then, softly: "I'm sorry about your father. I should've been there."

It hit me like a punch I hadn't seen coming. I nodded, but my throat was tight.

"I've always wanted to ask—why didn't you call me back? You knew how close I was with him. You liked him. It just felt like... you disappeared."

Her voice wavered. "I wanted to. But I was barely functioning. I was back in therapy, nearly took a leave from residency. Everything felt raw. Hearing about your dad just cracked it all open again. I didn't have anything left to give you."

I looked down at my shoes. "I would've taken anything. A voicemail. A text. Just to know you still cared."

She sighed. "It's my biggest regret. I failed you."

I didn't say anything. I didn't know how to make peace with something that had festered for so long. But I appreciated that she said it.

"I understand if you can't forgive me," she whispered.

"I'm not saying that. Just... I wanted to hear your voice. I needed something familiar when everything felt like it was falling apart."

I stepped closer. I didn't touch her. Just stood beside her.

"I've been thinking about that time a lot lately," she said. "About what we were. What we weren't. I don't know what to call this now. Do we need to rehash it all just to move on? Try to be friends? Pretend we're strangers with matching kids?"

Before I could answer, the door behind us opened and the circus spilled out.

Both boys were hyped, holding bonus Oreos like trophies. Alex already had chocolate on his sleeve. Mac blinked, pushing the emotion off her face like she'd snapped back into mom mode.

"Alex," she said brightly, "what did we say about asking your dad for extra dessert?"

"But Dad always says yes!" Alex grinned.

Mac rolled her eyes. Grace reached over to loop her arm through Mac's, already talking about throw pillows and wall hooks.

"Didn't you say you needed to go to the store first?" Mac asked her.

"I did. Let's go." They headed off toward the cars.

Alex looked horrified. "Dad, she's going to put me in a girly dorm room!"

David clapped him on the back. "We better go supervise, then. I want pictures."

"I'm riding with Mr. David this time, right?" Gabe called.

"Only if you beat me there!" Alex yelled back, taking off running.

I stood there a beat longer, watching them disappear into the sunset.

Mac's question still hung in the air.

What do we do now?

Whatever the answer was, it wasn't going to be simple. And it sure as hell wasn't going to be painless.

But maybe it was finally time to open the wound and clean it out — for good.

14

mackenzie

After Pink's, we made a quick stop at a nearby department store so Grace could grab a few last-minute things for Gabe's room.

According to Alex, we didn't need anything else, but I knew better. There's always something you forget when you're decorating a room. And if I happened to see a fluffy blanket or extra pillow that screamed *"mom cares"*, I wasn't walking out without it.

The men—both young and old—sent us in alone. Not the wisest decision. Honestly, it would've served them right if we came back with enough stuff to outfit the entire floor.

Grace had been nothing but kind to me since we met. Not just polite — kind. Warm. Easy. And I couldn't for the life of me figure out why.

If I were her? If I met the woman my ex-husband used to be in love with, the one he clearly still wasn't over... I don't think I'd be this friendly.
I'd met one or two of David's old flames over the years, but there was no love lost between us—we'd never been in love to begin with. So that was different. This felt more... *personal.*

As we pushed through the sliding doors, I glanced over at Grace. She was maybe 5'9", not quite as tall as me. Still clearly athletic—she'd mentioned track in college. She wore her curls short and natural. Light brown skin, a strong jawline, a quiet confidence. She was beautiful. Of course Evan had fallen for her.

Grace caught me looking. She didn't flinch.

"I bet you're wondering about me and Evan," she said, reaching for a shopping cart. "And why I've been nice to you."

I blinked, caught.

"I mean," she continued, steering us toward home goods, "it's not lost on me. If I were in your shoes, I'd probably be wondering too."

"That thought… had crossed my mind," I admitted.

She smiled, not smug, just understanding. "I don't hold my marriage to Evan against you. You weren't there. You weren't part of it. Besides, I always figured you and I would've been friends if we met under different circumstances—like during residency or something."

We stopped in front of a display of throw blankets. I picked up a white fluffy one that would go perfectly in Alex's room.

Grace reached out to touch it and grinned. "He's gonna lose it if you bring this into his space. But it's cute. If you want to start a war."

She kept browsing as we moved through the aisle.

"Evan was always honest about you," she said. "Not in a disrespectful way. He just… never really got over you. I used to blame him for that. But eventually, I realized—he didn't lie to me. I accepted a lot I shouldn't have. And that's on me."

I nodded, still processing her candor.

She held up a navy rug. "Thoughts?"

"Oh, I like that. Good call," I said, touching the fibers. "And sounds like you're no stranger to therapy, either."

Grace let out a short laugh. "Nope. Been there. Still there. And thank God for it."

She paused, then lowered her voice a little. "I've accepted a lot of shitty — excuse my French — behavior from men in my life. Evan wasn't one of those men, thankfully. He treated me well. But before him?" She took a deep breath. "I was raped in high school. By a guy I had a crush on. I spent years thinking it was my fault. Therapy helped me stop doing that."

Her face was calm, but I caught the faint flicker in her eyes. That pause that said she was still holding parts of it close. I knew that pause. I lived in it.

I swallowed. "I feel like I should apologize. For whatever fallout from Evan and I that landed in your lap. We never dealt with our shit properly. That must've bled into your life."

"There's no need," she said, grabbing a throw pillow — ruffled, of course — and holding it up.

I recoiled. "Absolutely not. Both boys would burn the place down."

She laughed and dropped it back in the bin.

Then her voice softened. "And speaking of deep-seated trauma…"

I gave her a look.

"Oh no," she said, raising an eyebrow. "You can't drop a line like *'I know about that'* and then move on. If we're building a friendship, I like to start from equal footing. Trauma bonding is the cornerstone of any good adult connection. What's your damage?"

I sighed. "Okay, but you asked." I paused, then: "My dad drowned saving me when I was five. My mom died from lupus when I was thirteen. My older brother blames me for both. He hasn't spoken to me in over twenty years."

Grace blinked once, then gave me a long look. "Damn," she whispered. Then she hooked her arm through mine. "I knew I liked you. We're gonna be just fine."

I shook my head, but I couldn't stop the smile tugging at the corner of my mouth.

"You may not see it yet," she continued, "but we're gonna be one big weird, messy, blended family one day. You, me, the boys, and the two idiots we married."

I raised an eyebrow. "What? Are you falling for David?"

She side-eyed me and smacked my shoulder. "Bitch."

We both broke into laughter.

"But seriously," I said, sobering a little. "Watch out for him. He's charming, flirty, multilingual… and full of shit."

Grace nodded thoughtfully. "Duly noted. Come on. Let's get out of here before the men come charging in, demanding we put back anything with a bow or a ruffle."

We made our way toward the checkout.

And I had to admit—she wasn't wrong.

We were definitely going to be friends.

Maybe not right now, but before it was all said and done for sure.

15

mackenzie

Decorating the rooms turned out to be a good time—at least for the moms.

I set up Alex's side of the room using the items I'd packed back in Atlanta. Despite my best efforts to stay out of the store with Grace, I somehow still managed to grab a few extras before we left. Nothing outrageous. Just enough to make it feel like home. Alex gave me the usual teenage side-eye when I started unpacking, but eventually, he admitted he liked it. The red, gray, and black combo worked. It was grown but still fun. The matching comforter and towels pulled it together, and the surprise swimming posters I'd tucked in my suitcase? Total win.

Gabe's room, on the other hand, looked like a blue-and-gold explosion. Grace went all out — bedding, towels, posters, even a matching trash can. Gabe and Alex were convinced she bought too much, but secretly? I think they loved it. And thankfully, the ruffly pillows she almost bought earlier stayed in the cart and out of their dorm.

We'd made a deal: if the boys got invited to stay for the longer program at the end of the week, we'd come back with reinforcements — and matching décor schemes.

While I was chatting with Grace and oohing over her color coordination, I noticed Evan and David talking off to the side. Evan kept glancing my way, pretending not to. Subtlety wasn't exactly his strength.

I didn't know what they were saying, but I caught snippets as I moved toward Gabe's desk: my name, the word *home*, something about *Alex*.

What exactly was Evan asking? And more importantly, why did I care? (Okay, I knew why I cared. But that was a rabbit hole I wasn't ready to spiral down.)

Once Alex was fully settled, David and I left Gabe and his parents to finish up. As we checked out at the dorm's front desk, David casually draped his arm across my shoulders.

I rolled it off without even looking up, which made the security attendant smirk.

"I know what you're doing," I said flatly, pushing open the door.

"It's fine. We used to be married," David joked, trailing after me like a loyal, unbothered shadow. "I was just kidding, *Guapa*! Don't be mad!"

I walked toward his Porsche without thinking.

"Wrong car," he said, amused. "Your Tahoe is in the lot."

I stopped in my tracks.

Damn it. I'd completely forgotten I drove myself here this morning. After everything with Evan, my brain had been running on autopilot.

I reached into my bag for the keys — and froze.

Double damn. I'd given them to Alex hours ago and still hadn't gotten them back.

I looked at my watch. Technically, curfew hadn't hit yet, but the thought of walking back inside to retrieve them? Nope. Not tonight. I was emotionally tapped out.

David, watching from the steps, tried — and failed — not to laugh. "Let me guess. Keys are in Alex's bag?"

I groaned.

"Maybe they'll let you back in—" he started.

I dropped my forehead onto the roof of his car. I had *one* vacation in years and somehow managed to regress into a flustered teenager with poor decision-making skills. All thanks to Evan.

"I'll take you back," David said, almost kindly. "We're at the same hotel anyway. I'll swing you back in the morning. Because I'm a good ex-husband. And because... you look a mess."

I braced myself for the ride back. David was about to get all the jokes off. And I couldn't even blame him. He'd warned me earlier today that I needed to talk to Evan — *really* talk to him.

And then Evan showed up like a walking memory with perfect skin and good intentions.

Of course I wasn't ready.

Of course I wanted to slap him.

Of course I also wanted to kiss him.

Which pissed me off. Not at him. Not even at David.

At myself — for still caring.

Being near Evan again had done something to me. Standing next to him outside Pink's, I caught a whiff of his cologne — different from what he used to wear, but still *him*. And suddenly, it was a decade ago, and I was a med student trying to keep my heart out of my pager.

David caught up to me as I stood silently fuming, and — because he's David — read me like a damn book.

"Stop looking at me like that," I snapped. "You *know* today was hard."

He leaned against the car. "Oh, I know. You've wanted to talk to him since the day we met. I saw your Grinch heart grow three sizes when y'all brushed hands earlier."

My eyes widened. "You were watching?"

"Of course I was. So was he."

He stepped forward, tone softening. "Mac, you gotta talk to him. For real. No middleman. No jokes. Just say what's been sitting in your chest for fifteen years."

I crossed my arms. "Why do you know me so well? Why couldn't I have married someone *oblivious*?"

He grinned. "Because deep down, you wanted someone who wouldn't let you bury your feelings under a five-year plan and a 'medium emotional distance' policy."

I sighed. "I'm still angry. Still sad. Still... confused."

"*Y enamorada.*" His voice was gentler now.

"I can't."

I moved to the passenger side door. "Let me in. My son ditched me, my ex is still fine, and I need junk food and minibar vodka to process my emotions."

David clicked the door open.

"You know," he said as we both got in, "you don't have to process those emotions alone. I'm just saying..."

I gave him a look.

"Thanks, but no thanks," I said. "And thank you. For being there. Even when I'm being a bitch."

"You're always a little bitchy," he said, smiling. "That's why I liked you."

I laughed as he started the engine.

He pulled away from the curb like it was just another day. But for me, the world felt off balance.

Somehow, Evan had pulled a piece of my heart to the surface, and I didn't know what to do with it yet.

16

mackenzie

The hotel room felt colder than I remembered. Still, I walked in and kicked off my shoes by the door. A single sock lay crumpled on the carpet just outside the bathroom — left over from earlier, I guessed. Somehow, it felt symbolic. Pathetic, but symbolic.

One lonely sock.

One very single me.

God.

I'd spent the last thirteen years making sure Alex had everything he needed — school, training, nutrition, transportation, dry towels. My calendar lived and died by his swim meets and tutoring schedules. I was the parent, the ride, the cheerleader, and the emergency contact. And now, he was in a dorm room I wouldn't see again until Saturday, thrilled to be on his own.

I was so used to being needed that I didn't even know what I wanted anymore. Not really.

When I was younger, I told myself I had to become a doctor. I owed it to my mother and grandmother to survive and be successful. And I did that. But I never stopped to ask myself if it was the life I *chose*, or the life I owed. Being with Evan was the first time I felt like I had a say in the matter — like maybe there was more to want than survival and sacrifice.

But after we broke up? After I buried that version of my future? I gave the reins right back. Got pregnant, got married, and poured myself into motherhood. It kept me distracted enough not to notice I'd stopped dreaming altogether.

Alex was my anchor. But he was also growing up. Leaving.

So, what now?

What did I want for *me*, now that the noise was fading?

I tossed my bag on the chair and made a beeline for the minibar. Chips. A candy bar. And a bourbon. I wasn't trying to be classy about it. I was trying to shut my brain off. The drink went down fast, and I refilled the glass with a splash of Coke to chase the fire. Then I sank into the couch and tried to get comfortable, but the silence kept poking at me. This room felt too still. Like it knew I was hiding.

And that sock was still just... there. Mocking me.

Right when I started considering a second bourbon, my phone rang from somewhere across the room. Of course. I sighed, got up, and passed the sock again.

It was Adrienne — Dr. Adrienne Graves, but I'd never called her that in my life. Ree had been in my study group during med school, back before life got too real. We lost touch for a while, but reconnected a few years after residency. Now she was one of the only people who could call me out without pissing me off. Usually.

"Hey, Ree," I sniffled, flopping back onto the bed like I had the weight of the world in my bones. Miraculously, I didn't spill my bourbon. "How are you?"

"*Giiiiirrrrl.* I just finished a 24-hour NICU shift. My feet hurt. My soul hurts. I poured a wine the size of my face." She took a loud gulp. "But I remembered today's the day. Swim Academy. Miami. You're sitting there with bourbon and carbs, questioning all your life choices, right?"

I looked around the room.

She wasn't wrong.

"Alex is officially dormed up," I said, dragging a pillow over my lap. "So I'm alone, buzzed, and having an existential crisis. But I *do* have news."

"Ooooh," she said, already intrigued. "Give it to me."

"You'll never guess who's here."

A pause. "Don't do this. Don't make me guess."

"Evan."

Clunk.

Something dropped. I waited.

"Evan? *Evan* Evan?" she sputtered. "Evan Robertson?! He has a kid?! You didn't know?!?"

"Yes to all the above." I rubbed my temples. "He's here. Still absurdly fine. Has a little salt-and-pepper thing happening. And a twelve-year-old son. Alex and Gabe became best friends before I could even blink."

"You're lying. Tell me you talked."

"Some. Enough to make me want to cry or throw up. Possibly both."

Ree took another gulp. "Mac. This is your second chance."

"I don't know if I want a second chance."

"You *do*. You're just scared."

I stared at the ceiling, trying not to picture Evan's face. "We're not the same people."

"You're not supposed to be," Ree shot back. "You're supposed to be older and smarter. Less reactive. More... grown."

"That's generous of you."

Ree ignored the sarcasm. "Look, you've been alone a long time. You don't even date."

"I *had* a toddler," I protested. "And a full-time job."

"And now you have a teenage swimmer in a dorm and a drawer full of toys at home."

"Two, actually. Drawers, I mean."

"Exactly my point."

I laughed despite myself. "I can't believe I'm doing this. Bourbon and ex-boyfriends and vibrator confessions. I'm officially forty."

"You are." I heard her wine glass hit the table again. "And you're still in love with the man. So figure it out before the universe yanks him away again."

That shut me up.

And it stuck.

We hung up a few minutes later, with Ree swearing she wouldn't remember anything she said, and me wondering if maybe that was for the best.

Even tipsy, I couldn't stop thinking.

The first time Evan and I fell apart, it was a hundred little things. A bad recipe of distance, ambition, stress, and pride. He couldn't always call. I couldn't always stay calm. The tension between us built until everything broke at once — my trust, his patience, our connection.

Then his father died, and I made the biggest mistake of all: I didn't call back. I disappeared.

Now here we were again, years later, our kids sleeping in twin beds down the road. And I had no idea how to move forward—how to close the gap between what we were and what we might be. I went to my suitcase and unzipped a smaller pouch, pulling out my mini-wand. If I couldn't figure out what to do emotionally, I could at least get some endorphins going. I lay back on the bed, vibrator in hand, and tried not to think too hard.

But even as my body relaxed and the bourbon softened everything around the edges, one thing stayed sharp:

I missed him.

I missed *us*.

And for the first time in a long time, I was starting to wonder what it might look like to want something for myself again.

Even if it scared the hell out of me.

17

evan

I needed to talk this through with someone. Someone not here. Someone not emotionally entangled in all of this. Which meant not Grace, and definitely not David.

That left me with two options: Liza — my older sister — or Victor, Grace's brother. Victor and I had stayed friends after the divorce, even though that was dicey for a while. He'd always said Grace and I didn't really fit. Not romantically, anyway. He supported her, of course, but he was vocal about his reservations even back then. Said he'd be there when it all went to hell. And he was. Funny enough, he'd known about Mac long before I ever mentioned her. Grace talked about her too — *that* kind of story sticks in a marriage. At some point, Victor made it clear he thought I needed to get back with Mac just so everyone could finally shut up about it. Himself included.

He wasn't wrong.

But that wasn't the energy I needed tonight. I needed someone who knew me better. So I called Liza.

She picked up on the first ring. "Hello, stranger."

I rolled my eyes. "We talked two days ago."

"You're in Florida. I assumed I'd be getting a full report by now. Swim camp, teenage bonding, sunshine..."

"I've been... distracted."

That got her attention. The line went quiet.

"What happened?" she asked slowly. "Is everyone okay?"

I paused. "Yes. Grace and Gabe are fine."

A beat. Then— "Ouch. Sorry. Eliana's feeding. Her gums are murder right now. But go on."

I frowned. Of course she was nursing. My niece was barely a month old. "Listen, I didn't mean to call during baby time."

"Evan, just say what happened."

I took a breath.

"Mac's here."

I heard a thump and a long stream of chaos — muffled yelling, footsteps, and our mom's voice somewhere in the background insisting Liza was perfectly capable of handling a phone while breastfeeding.

Then Mom picked up.

"Hi, son. How's the Academy? How's my excellent grandson?"

"He's great. But I really need to finish talking to Liza before she combusts."

Mom chuckled. "Alright, but you owe me a call tomorrow. I want details."

"I promise."

Eventually, Liza came back on, breathless. "You're telling me Mackenzie is in Miami. At the *same* camp. With her son."

"Yeah."

"I should fly down there and slap you for not opening with that."

"I didn't think you wanted updates *that* badly."

"Don't play with me, Evan. What happened?"

I told her the basics — where we were staying, how we ran into each other, how our sons met first and hit it off like they'd known each other for years. How it's been awkward and raw and quiet and emotional all at once.

By the time I finished, Liza was quiet.

"You okay?" I asked.

"I'm just trying to decide how honest to be right now."

"That bad?"

"Not bad. Just... real." She took a breath. "Are you going to try again?"

"I don't know."

"Don't give me that."

"I'm serious, Liza. She and I haven't had an actual conversation. We've spoken, sure. We've been… near each other. But it's been fifteen years. We're not the same people."

"No. You're not. But that's not a bad thing." She paused. "You still love her?"

I didn't answer.

"She still looks good?"

I laughed quietly. "She looks incredible. Still tall. Still gorgeous. She's wearing contacts now. Started swimming herself. Her posture's better. She walks like she owns the place."

Liza hummed. "So, yes. You're cooked."

"I just think we should start by being friends again. That might be all we can manage."

"You're lying to yourself, but fine." She wasn't being judgmental. She was being my sister. "Have you told her how you felt back then? How you feel now?"

"No."

"Then you're still doing the same thing you did fifteen years ago. You avoid the mess. You try to fix everything around the edges and hope it gets better on its own."

That stung.

Because it was true.

"You have one week," she said. "One. If you walk away without even trying, you'll regret it."

"I'm scared she'll leave again."

"Then you're human. But fear doesn't make the decision for you, Evan. You do."

She sighed. "I've got to go. Eliana's done feeding, and she smells suspicious. Call me tomorrow. And tell Mom something vague so she doesn't start planning a wedding."

"I'll think about it."

"You always do. That's your problem." She hung up.

I sat on the edge of the hotel bed and stared at my phone.

Liza was right. If I kept doing what I've always done — avoiding, deflecting, rationalizing — I was going to lose Mackenzie all over again.

And this time?

There wouldn't be another chance.

18

evan

When the alarm went off at 5:30 AM, I didn't move at first. For a split second, I expected to hear footsteps — maybe a sleepy twelve-year-old grumbling about getting up for practice. But the room was silent. He wasn't here. And neither was his mother.

That stung more than I wanted to admit.

My next thought was Mac. Seeing her yesterday cracked open something I'd boarded up a long time ago. It wasn't just the big things I remembered — it was small flashes. Early mornings in bed, untouched by our hospital shifts. A weekend in Memphis. That picnic in the courtyard, back when we still thought we had time to slow down. I let the memories wash over me, uninvited but persistent.

A little voice whispered: *You could still have the real thing.*

Eventually, I hauled myself out of bed. Threw on my swim trunks, grabbed a towel, and headed out. My body was craving the water. Yesterday's tour left no time for laps, and when I asked the guide if I could use the pool, he shut it down quick. So today, I made my own plan: thirty minutes every morning. No excuses.

At the front desk, I asked the overnight attendant, "Is the pool open this early?"

He eyed me like I'd asked to take the elevator to Mars. "Yeah, but I hope you're a strong swimmer."

I didn't bother responding. He followed me to the pool, flicked on the lights, and pointed to the 'No Lifeguard on Duty' sign like I'd missed it.

I nodded, dropped my towel, and dove in clean. Freestyle. No hesitation. After a few laps, I heard the door close behind him.

Underwater, I let the strokes carry me, my mind drifting where it wanted. Mostly to Mac. Fifteen years is a long time, but some things don't leave you. The lack of contact after my father died — no call, no message — still sat heavy. Back then, I swore it was unforgivable. Maybe it was. But now? I wasn't sure I could say that with conviction.

I swam for thirty minutes before heading back up. The desk clerk looked almost relieved to see me walking. Probably didn't want to end his shift fishing a middle-aged man out of the deep end.

In my room, I started the sad little one-cup coffee maker and flipped on the news. Shower. Clothes. Coffee in a travel cup. Keys. Out the door. I'd bet money I was the last to arrive.

I was right.

Grace waved me over as I entered the natatorium. I saw Mac glance my way, then quickly turn, the oversized sunglasses making it hard to read her. Still, she looked well-rested or at least like she wanted people to think she was.

I sat next to Grace. "Alright. What'd I miss?"

"Nothing big," she said quietly. "The head of the academy spoke, someone else will wrap it up. We'll get breakfast, come back, and later—some time with the boys."

I nodded, then hesitated. "So, uh, what's the plan for today? I mean, I assumed Mac and David wanted to spend time with us... but they might have their own plans."

Grace smirked. "Not just them. Maybe *I* don't want to spend the day with you."

She tried to keep the joke light, but it flickered—grimace instead of grin.

Before I could ask what was wrong, I noticed Mac covering her face, shoulders shaking with laughter. Then she stopped, leaned forward, hand on her forehead like the motion itself was a risk.

David spoke up. "Ignore her. She's got a hangover."

I glanced back at Mac. For someone hungover, she looked incredible. Which, of course, led me to wonder why she got drunk in the first place. Celebration? Nerves? Us?

David continued, "We'll all probably spend time together this week. Get used to it. I'll be the coolest man both our kids will ever know."

I chuckled. "Hard to argue with that."

He added, "The boys want to hit the beach tonight before curfew kicks in. So, we'll head out right after they're dismissed."

Mac elbowed him.

"Oh, yeah, we gotta run by the store first. Pick up a few things to apologize for the glitter bomb that is their dorm room," he said.

Mac jabbed him again. Harder. Grace and I both laughed.

Still, Grace kept her hand on her stomach. I leaned in. "Is your stomach acting up again?"

She nodded faintly. "I'm okay. Just don't want to throw things off."

I remembered her old GI flares—stress always triggered them.

The director of training stood to speak, offering the usual encouragements to parents and cautions for the kids. I'd heard it before—thirty years ago, when I was the twelve-year-old sitting here. Back when I thought I was headed for Olympic glory. Distance races. Big dreams.

Life had other plans.

I drifted into the memory, wondering what success in that version of my life might have looked like. No med school. No Mac. No Gabe.

Maybe missing out was the win.

Someone tapped my shoulder.

Mac.

She stepped back slightly after I turned. "David and Grace went to say goodbye to the boys."

"You didn't?"

"I talked to Alex earlier. He called at 5:15 this morning super excited, also holding my car keys hostage."

She winced. "The call didn't do my hangover any favors. But at least I got to hear his voice."

"Thanks for waiting." I paused. "I remember breakfast was mentioned?"

Even now, I felt the pull to reach for her like maybe if I touched her hand, this thing between us would make sense again. But I didn't.

I couldn't.

She gave me a small, almost bashful smile. "When they're done, we're going to Miam Café. You know I love breakfast."

"I remember."

"Hopefully some carbs can cure this headache."

"Celebrating something last night?" I asked.

She gave me a look — half-knowing, half-deflecting. "Why would you assume I was celebrating?"

And then, just like that, we were standing in the middle of years. All of it. The good. The painful. The unsaid.

I wanted to say something. I really did.

But she looked away first.

"Come on," she said, pointing toward Grace and Gabe. "You should go say goodbye. I think Grace is trying to smother him."

We walked over. Gabe looked nervous, and for a moment, I felt it too. Maybe I'd made the wrong call sending him here.

Then he looked up at me, and I saw it. That spark. That quiet strength. He was my kid through and through.

"You ready to show them what you've got?" I asked.

"Yup," he grinned. "I'm gonna earn that Poseidon tattoo you promised me!"

Grace whipped around, glare sharp enough to cut glass. That tattoo promise had been a running battle between us—but it gave Gabe confidence. I'd take the heat later.

He walked off, head high, and for the first time in a while, I let myself believe he'd be okay.

Maybe it was time I stopped letting fear make all my decisions.

19

grace

By the time I slid into Evan's Tahoe for the ride to breakfast, I already regretted leaving the hotel. The nausea had hit in waves all morning, and now it was settling in for the long haul. I leaned my head back against the seat and tried not to breathe too deep.

Still—this breakfast mattered. For Mac. For Evan. For all of us, really. If I didn't set something in motion now, it might never happen.

David was behind the wheel, humming along to the radio. I asked about the restaurant, hoping food talk would distract me.

He perked up immediately. "They've got everything. French toast, croissants, café con leche, smoked salmon, these guava pastries that'll change your life—"

"You clearly love this place," I muttered, eyes closed.

"Every time I'm in Miami. Non-negotiable."

"Of course it is." I groaned under my breath. The descriptions sounded amazing. Which only made me feel worse.

I glanced behind us. Mac was curled into the corner of the second row, dozing with her sunglasses still on. Evan sat beside her, quiet, eyes fixed out the window. They weren't talking. Barely even looking at each other.

Perfect.

I turned back to David. "Now's a good time. They're out cold."

He gave me a warning look, then held up his phone, thumb hovering over the volume. "If they catch on, I'm blaming you."

"Blame away," I said, waving him off. "But we need to talk strategy. They're not going to figure this out on their own."

David chuckled, but there was an edge of agreement. "You're really serious about this matchmaking thing, huh?"

"Dead serious. And don't act surprised. I've always wanted to moonlight as a private investigator. This is the next best thing."

"You know if this backfires, we're both in trouble."

"Absolutely. But if we don't try, they'll leave here exactly the way they came—frustrated, bitter, and pretending like fifteen years didn't happen." I pressed a hand to my stomach as it clenched again. "Which will make the rest of this trip hell for all of us."

He gave me a sidelong glance. "You sure you're okay?"

"Nope," I muttered. "Reflux. I left my meds on the dresser."

"Damn. You want to skip breakfast?"

"I'm skipping food either way. But let's at least get them to the café. Then I'll head back to the hotel."

David looked skeptical. "You really think leaving them alone is a good idea?"

I sighed. "No clue. But we're not going to get a confession of love if we're sitting at the table with them. We give them space. Maybe they actually say what they need to say."

He hesitated. "You think they still want that? Each other?"

"I think they're scared," I said quietly. "And tired. But yeah... I think the door's still cracked open. Someone just has to push it."

We pulled up next to a parked car. David shifted into park.

"Alright," I said before he could talk me out of it. "Let's wake the sleeping beauties and get this show on the road. I've got meds to take and a bed calling my name."

He laughed, but it sounded like nerves. "You're relentless, you know that?"

"Damn right."

20

mackenzie

By the time we pulled away from the Academy, none of us had much to say. The Tahoe ride was quiet—no sarcastic jabs, no passive commentary. Just four parents sitting in a vehicle, all a little hollow from leaving our boys behind. The silence felt heavier than usual.

My headache had dulled after the Tylenol, but the ache behind my eyes lingered, a reminder not to drown my emotions in brown liquor. I should've known better. I *do* know better. But yesterday hit me harder than I expected.

David and Grace took the front seats, Evan and I sat in the second row. I leaned my head back and closed my eyes. Not to sleep, not really. Just to retreat.

The next time I opened them, we were double-parked outside the café.

Grace and I went inside while the men circled to find parking. Or so I thought.

The smell inside Miam Café Wynwood hit me instantly — warm bread, syrup, coffee. My stomach grumbled in response. As I've gotten older, I've tried to be more mindful about indulgence. Pancakes today meant an extra mile tomorrow. But this place? Worth it.

Grace stood beside me at the hostess stand, menu in hand. She looked pale, and the menu wasn't helping.

"The salmon toast is calling my name," she muttered. "But my stomach's not cooperating. Stress gets my GI tract every time. Irony of being a GI doc with reflux, right?"

I smiled sympathetically. "I get it. Every time Alex had a fever or a rash or anything, I felt like I was failing—both as a mother and a pediatrician."

She winced again, and this time it wasn't from laughter. "Seriously, are you going to be okay? We can just get food to go."

Truthfully, I hadn't expected to feel so comfortable with the woman who used to be married to my ex-fiancé. But Grace? She was easy to talk to. It was the rest of this — *him* — that left me feeling exposed.

Grace looked at me, eyes direct. "I'm not sure I'll make it through breakfast, to be honest. I left my meds at the hotel. But before I leave... I want to ask you for something."

I narrowed my eyes slightly, instinct already bracing for what was coming.

"I want you and Evan to talk. Actually talk. Not five minutes of polite avoidance, not sidelong glances. A real conversation. I want to enjoy the rest of this trip. And until you two clear the air, we're all holding our breath."

And just like that, the anxiety crept back in.

I didn't argue — because she was right. We'd been orbiting each other all week, pretending things were casual when nothing about our past — or this moment — was.

She saw the shift in my face, but she didn't flinch.

"I'm not trying to push you into anything painful," she added gently. "But it's been fifteen years. You both deserve peace."

Evan and David walked in then. The timing was too perfect. I knew exactly what was happening.

Evan came to stand beside me, unaware of the plan that had just unfolded. I turned toward David and pulled him aside.

"I can't believe you're doing this," I whispered.

David shrugged. "Y'all are gonna have to sit still and talk eventually. You had your shot after Big Pink's and dodged it. Now? We're done pretending. Your unresolved drama is ruining my beach vibe."

"And you think *this* is the solution?" I asked, incredulous.

He grinned. "Hey, it can't get worse." Then, without giving me room to argue, he kissed my cheek and followed Grace out the door.

I glared after them. "Reflux," I muttered. "Sure."

I turned to Evan. He looked as confused as I felt.

"Well," I said, trying not to look directly at him. "Looks like we've been abandoned."

He nodded, eyes scanning me in a way I recognized immediately.

And just like that, the tension was back.

My nerves kicked in. I bit my lip — a habit I'd never fully broken. His gaze flicked downward, and I saw it. That shift. That hunger. He didn't bother disguising it. His eyes moved over me slowly, like memory, pausing in all the places he used to claim. Neck. Chest. Hips.

It was a lot.

Too much.

We were in trouble.

The hostess returned and led us to a small table on the patio. Quiet. Out of the way. Like she sensed we had history to unravel.

"Weren't there four of you?" she asked, glancing around.

"They didn't feel well," Evan said, placing his hand gently on the small of my back. The contact sent heat through me — familiar and unwelcome.

As we sat, I ordered a latte. Evan smiled knowingly.

"Still drinking one every morning, huh?"

"Most mornings. Yesterday was an exception. Too wired."

"I used to think you ordered them just to be difficult."

I raised an eyebrow. "And now?"

He smiled faintly. "Some things change."

There it was. The shift. The reminder. We'd both changed.

The server took our orders — tres leches pancakes for me, granola and French toast for him.

Once she left, Evan cleared his throat. "So... we've been set up."

"Clearly."

"I guess we're supposed to clear the air."

I gave a wry smile. "Think we can manage that over waffles?"

"We can try. You were my best friend once."

I tilted my head. "You told me you wanted me the first time you saw me."

"I did. But we were friends first."

I thought back to those early months. Study sessions. Late-night conversations. Our first real kiss after weeks of dancing around each other. Yeah, we were friends. Until we weren't.

"We were solid until we didn't match together," I said softly.

He nodded but held up a hand as the food arrived. "Before we dive in... I want to say this."

I looked up.

"I'm sorry, Mac. For how I handled everything. When I left for San Francisco, I didn't try hard enough. I got wrapped up in my program, in my ego. I should've prioritized *us*. But I didn't. That's on me."

His voice didn't waver. He meant it.

I let out a slow breath. "You're not the only one who failed us. I let my insecurities run the show. I assumed the worst. Believed I didn't deserve you. I spiraled."

"You were never a burden."

"You say that now, but back then... I couldn't risk hearing otherwise. I went back to therapy. Tried to rebuild my sense of self. I needed space."

He nodded. "I just wish I'd known. I wish you'd told me."

"I couldn't. Because if I heard your voice, I would've gone back. No hesitation."

"Would that have been so bad?"

I looked down at my untouched plate. "Maybe not. But I wasn't healthy. And I didn't want to drag you into that."

His eyes were soft. "You wouldn't have."

One tear slipped down my cheek before I could stop it. I brushed it away quickly.

"I don't want to go through all the old wounds," I said. "Not again. We hurt each other. That's the truth. And we both survived."

He nodded.

"So what now?" I asked.

"We try being friends?" Evan offered.

It sounded weak coming out. Like a compromise neither of us believed.

He reached out his hand. I took it. His fingers lingered longer than necessary, trailing across my palm as he let go. I shivered.

Friends. Sure.

I pointed to the food. "It's getting cold."

"I'm starving," he said, grabbing his fork.

I watched him dig into his granola like it personally offended him. I couldn't eat. My appetite had vanished somewhere between "sorry" and "you were never a burden."

I flagged the server. Asked for boxes.

We had our answer, I guess.

He wanted clean lines. Friendship. Closure.

But my heart had been hoping for something else.

I took a sip of my now-cold latte. Bitter. Like this conversation.

Friends, I repeated to myself.

But I already knew better.

21

evan

I couldn't believe what had just come out of my mouth.

Friends?

Friends?

Was I high?

I said it like I meant it — like I hadn't just watched her nearly cry across the table. Like I didn't still want her in ways that didn't fit neatly into a friendship box. But I'd panicked — defaulted to safe. I didn't want to push her too hard. Not yet.

Still, I recognized the look on her face the moment I said it. Fifteen years apart and I could still read her that easily. That flicker of disappointment? Yeah. She'd been hoping for something more.

And I shut it down.

I started eating — fast — like the granola might distract me from how stupid I felt. She didn't even touch her food. Just stared for a minute, then quietly asked for boxes. She was already halfway out of the conversation. I didn't blame her.

Whatever Grace and David had hoped this breakfast would accomplish — it didn't land. I'd wanted to crack the door open again. Instead, I slammed it shut myself.

Grace was going to kill me.

Now I'd boxed myself in. I couldn't backpedal, not without making it worse. I'd have to be careful — intentional. Maybe I could still salvage this. Ease the door open a little at a time.

Five days. That's what I had.

After I paid, we stepped outside only to realize neither of us had a ride. David and Grace were long gone. It was barely 10 AM.

"We can call an Uber if you want to head back to your hotel," Mac said. Her voice was even. Neutral. She was already pulling away.

But I wasn't ready for this to be over — not yet.

"I don't want to go back yet," I said. "Do you know what area we're in?"

She gave me a look. "You mean Wynwood? The mural district? All the building art?"

Right. Of course she knew. I should've remembered she'd been here before. That pang of jealousy hit quick — sharp. I reminded myself that she was allowed to have a life outside of me. *Had* to, really.

Luckily, she didn't seem to notice the thoughts running wild behind my eyes.

"I love this neighborhood," she said. "I thought about bringing Alex down here once. There's enough color and energy to keep any twelve-year-old interested. Gabe might like to see it — especially if you call it graffiti instead of art."

I smiled. "That's actually a good idea. We'll have to check the schedule. Grace would probably enjoy it too."

"You want to walk for a bit?" she asked. "There are a few great walls up ahead."

"Yeah. Let's."

We walked slowly, food containers in hand, letting the morning unfold without too much pressure. Mac pointed out pieces along the buildings — explaining how artists were paid to do full murals, how some were several stories high or hidden until you turned the right corner. It wasn't just impressive — it was alive. The way she lit up as she explained it reminded me of the old days — lazy weekends at art museums or city parks, whenever we managed a few hours off together.

I had to reel myself back in.

"I'm rambling," she said suddenly. "There's a graffiti museum nearby. A hip-hop museum too. I just... I think I'm talking because I'm nervous. Trying to figure out how to be friends with you again."

I appreciated the honesty. "It's weird," I admitted. "But yeah — it's just going to take a minute. We weren't nothing, Mac."

She stopped walking. Turned toward me.

"You've been imprinted on my heart and soul, Evan. You'll always be there. But maybe now — maybe this time — it can be healthier. Less what-ifs. Less pain."

Something about the word *imprinted* stayed with me. She was right. She was part of me, always had been. No amount of silence or time apart had changed that.

We kept walking.

Apparently, Grace and David hadn't planned to leave us stranded forever. I guess our radio silence after breakfast made them antsy, because a black Tahoe rolled up beside us not long after. We were standing in front of a mural of a bold, half-naked woman with wild colors swirling around her. Grace leaned out the window.

"Hey! What are you two doing out here? That painting is incredible. Also — I see to-go boxes. Did you even eat?"

"You set us up to talk," Mac said with a raised eyebrow. "I didn't exactly have time to eat my tres leches pancakes."

Grace looked sheepish, which was rare. David leaned across her.

"Y'all done? I want to catch the swim session. And for the record, Grace and I *did* eat — though hers looked like medical-grade paste."

"It was yogurt," Grace huffed. "And it helped. Unlike whatever you two ordered and wasted."

I opened the back door and held it for Mac before sliding in after her. "Leaving us stranded wasn't as subtle as you think."

"I *actually* have stomach issues," Grace said, giving me a sharp look. "Are you two getting along better?"

"For now," I said, keeping my tone even.

Mac smiled, catching my meaning. We weren't giving them anything. They wanted a success story — they could wait.

David drove us back to the Academy just in time for the mid-morning swim session. Grace spent the entire ride complaining about us trying to eat syrup-covered carbs in the back seat. She wasn't wrong — pancakes and French toast don't travel well. I was going to need to wipe down the seats before I returned the rental if I didn't want a cleaning fee.

And yet... that 30-minute ride was the most relaxed I'd felt around Mac since we reunited. Something had shifted. Maybe not entirely healed, but loosened. We laughed. Passed each other bites of food like we used to. When I gave her a piece of my French toast, she smiled at me — wide, warm, real.

That smile felt like we *could* be friends.

But the way her eyes lingered?

That told a different story.

22

grace

The midday swim session had the kids grouped by skill level, alternating between sprints and relay drills. It was surprisingly engrossing — technical, focused, competitive. I'd just started mentally breaking down one swimmer's turn technique when my phone buzzed in my pocket.

David

Meet me by the concession stand.

Of course.

I glanced at him, eyebrow raised, then gestured subtly toward the pool. He shook his head and stood, weaving his way through the bleachers like this was a mission. Typical.

Mac and Evan noticed him leave but didn't say anything. They were too focused on the lanes. I waited a few minutes before standing and muttering something about needing water.

David was waiting near the snack counter, halfway through a candy bar. He held it out as I approached — like that was supposed to tempt me.

I shook my head. "If I even look at that too long, my stomach's going to revolt."

He grinned. "More for me."

"How do you stay in shape eating like that?" I asked, grabbing a bottle of water.

"Good genes. Former athlete advantage. And according to you, I'm still in shape?"

I gave him a look. "Don't fish."

"Noted," he said, eyes still amused. Then, finally shifting gears, "I wanted a quick check-in. See where we stand on Operation: Reconciliation. Breakfast seemed... promising?"

"They won't tell us anything directly," I said, taking a sip. "But yeah — the ice has definitely thawed."

"I saw it too. Mac was actually talking about the pancakes. And your boy's French toast."

"She sounded a little flirty."

"You jealous?" he asked, mostly teasing.

"Years ago, maybe. Now? I want Evan happy. If it's with her, even better."

David nodded. "Same. Mac and I — that was never romantic. We were good teammates. But I think she needs something that's... hers. Something real. And Evan still gets under her skin in a way no one else does."

"She loves him," I said quietly. "Even if she doesn't want to."

"She's scared to want anything for herself," David replied. "That's been true since the divorce."

I sighed. "So, what's our next play?"

He raised a brow. "Key West. Overnight. Just the two of them. No distractions."

"Wednesday?"

"Wednesday. They need a couple more days to stop overthinking everything."

"And tomorrow?" I asked.

"Little Havana. I need good Cuban food. And coffee. The real kind — not the watered-down hotel stuff."

I smiled. "You've got tomorrow planned out already?"

"I do. I'll send you the itinerary later. But for Wednesday — I'll make sure Mac and Evan don't bail. I'm thinking reservations, activities, and maybe no easy way back without staying overnight."

"Strategic sabotage. I like it."

"And we get a full day to ourselves. Win-win."

I gave him a look. "Let's be clear — I know what that wink means, and this is not *that*. There will be no 'private time.'"

He held up his hands, mock-innocent. "Mac warned you about me?"

"She did."

"She's dramatic."

"You're *you*. And you're exactly the kind of man I'd make a terrible decision with."

That got his attention.

I followed with, "Which is why we're staying friends. I've got someone back home. Nothing serious yet, but serious enough. I'm not trying to cross any lines."

David nodded, backing off with grace I hadn't expected. "I don't mess with married women or women in relationships. You're safe. But — just for the record — you'd be missing out."

I rolled my eyes but didn't answer. Truth was, I *could* make a mistake here if I wasn't careful. He was charming, self-aware, and incredibly easy to talk to. But I knew better.

And when you know better — you do better.

We realized we'd missed most of the session and made our way back to the bleachers.

Neither Evan nor Mac looked up as we returned. But I did notice they were sitting closer — their thighs actually touching now.

I glanced over at David and tilted my head toward the pair.

We were definitely on the right track.

23

mackenzie

Once David and Grace returned from their mysterious mission, we watched the rest of the swimming session. It lasted maybe another twenty minutes. Afterward, the parents had a few minutes to check in with their swimmers before the kids headed to lunch.

Gabe was practically vibrating when he ran over to hug Evan and Grace. His words tumbled over one another.

"I got to show the coach my freestyle — he said my stroke looked really good! I can't believe it. He actually likes what he sees, so far!"

That kind of early feedback? It meant everything to Gabe. You could see it all over his face.

Alex was just as happy to see David and me, though I quickly realized it had less to do with missing us and more to do with everything else going on.

Apparently, he and Gabe had already made friends with their roommates — and with at least one other person.

"Alex has a new friend," Gabe said casually, clearly enjoying the stir. "A girl."

I turned to stare at my son. He gave me a sheepish grin. David, meanwhile, gave him a high five.

My baby — trying to chat up a girl?

A few seconds later, said girl came strolling over. Tall, poised, beautiful brown skin, and 13 years old — like Alex. She looked like she belonged on a track team *and* in a catalog. I kept my expression neutral as she offered a polite smile.

"Mom, Dad — this is Skylar. She's from Colorado," Alex said.

David shook her hand. "What's your specialty?"

"I'm a sprinter," she answered, respectful and confident.

I was proud to see another young Black girl out here — one of the few. But the mom in me still panicked. This was a new phase, and I wasn't quite ready to see my son walking into it.

After introductions, the boys went off to lunch. The adults grabbed tacos from a drive-thru and agreed to head back to our rooms to rest before the evening beach trip. The boys were excited — something about sunset photos and playing in the waves hit that perfect middle-school sweet spot.

I was so hungry, I started eating in the SUV again. I'd probably end up helping clean this rental if we didn't want a surcharge. Once we got to my hotel, David started in immediately.

"So... what did you and Evan talk about?"

I ignored him and disappeared into the bathroom.

"I'm serious!" he called. "Was it good? Productive?"

"I'm going to shower and take a nap," I yelled back. "Not debriefing you right now. But thanks for playing matchmaker."

I peeked out the door just long enough to catch him mocking me in a high-pitched voice before flipping on the TV and finishing off his food.

I changed into a two-piece and a white cover-up, tossed my hair into a loose bun, and collapsed onto my bed. I was too tired to care how I looked — or whether Evan would care, either.

We were just friends now, right?

I set my alarm for 5:00. I was out in seconds.

When I woke up and walked into the living room, David was knocked out on the couch, legs draped across the arm like a teenager. I paused for a moment, watching him.

As frustrating as David could be, I couldn't imagine my life if I hadn't bumped into him in Vegas that day. For better or worse, we'd built something real — co-parenting, friendship, trust. He always had Alex's back. And mine, even when I didn't ask for it.

To show my appreciation, I kicked the edge of the couch.

He jolted awake, mumbling in half-asleep Spanish. "Bella... no te vayas, déjame abrazarte."

Ugh. I did *not* want to know what that dream was about.

"David. Wake up. We've got to go."

"Sorry! Guapa, I was — uh — just resting my eyes." He sat up fast, clearly trying to recalibrate.

I got an unfortunate flash of what the problem had been and quickly turned around.

"Mmhm. Business handled, I hope?" I muttered.

With his hands strategically placed, he shuffled off to the bathroom.

I shook my head.

Our friendship defied all definitions. Too close? Probably. Would that be a problem for anyone I tried to build a future with — Evan included?

I didn't have the answer. Not yet.

But I knew one thing — Evan had said the word *friends* that morning, and I was still trying to figure out how I felt about it. Maybe the beach would give us a chance to clear the air.

Alex and Gabe were waiting by the dorm's front desk when we arrived. Both had changed into hoodies and jean shorts — eager, antsy, full of questions about the beach. They sat in the third row of the Tahoe and immediately began peppering us with nonstop commentary.

Grace, of course, had once again claimed the front seat "for reflux," which meant Evan and I were back in the second row. At this point, I was convinced they were orchestrating the entire seating arrangement.

Gabe had more beach experience, having grown up in California. Alex had only vague memories. The entire ride became a chorus of questions and facts — Alex asking something, Gabe chiming in, one of us adults answering in the front, then another question coming right after.

Any chance of a real conversation with Evan disappeared under the noise.

At one point, a car swerved out in front of us. David slammed the brakes. Instinctively, Evan threw his arm across my chest.

"Are you okay?" he asked, his voice low.

I nodded, startled by the gesture — not because I needed it, but because it came so naturally to him.

David, meanwhile, was cursing in Spanish with the kind of fluency only earned through years of multilingual arguments. Alex started translating for Gabe.

Grace, intrigued, made David repeat the phrases slowly so she could memorize the pronunciation.

"Planning to curse people out fluently in Spanish now?" I asked, raising an eyebrow.

"Absolutely," she replied.

David explained the mix of dialects — Spain, the Caribbean, Central America. He had family scattered across all of them. The combination was... colorful.

"Let's just remember there are impressionable ears in the back," I said.

Alex — ever helpful — tried to reassure me. "I already know what those words mean, Mom. I'm only explaining the age-appropriate ones to Gabe."

David narrowed his eyes. "Which ones are those?"

"You remember! The ones you taught me when I was eleven. They are —"

"That's fine. No need to repeat," David cut in quickly. "Let's keep that our little secret."

Grace and I both punched him in the arm.

"Hey! This is my money maker!" he protested. "Right-handed shooter over here!"

"Not in the league right now," I said flatly.

I turned to Evan. "He's not in the league right now."

Evan laughed. "You're relentless."

David dropped into an exaggerated old man voice. "Just wait. I'll show you. I've still got it!"

We were all still laughing when he pulled into the lot near the beach.

"And I'll be here all week..." David added. "Ba-dum-bum."

I hadn't been back to Miami Beach since my marriage. After my father's accident at Gulf Shores, I'd avoided the ocean completely. Evan was the one who slowly brought me back to the water — vacation by vacation, until I could stand in the waves without falling apart.

David picked up where Evan left off. He brought Alex here when he was still a baby — little hands full of sand, giggling at the foam. And somehow, I joined in, feet buried in the shoreline, wondering how I'd gotten brave enough to stand there again.

Tonight, the breeze was perfect. Warm. The water glowed with the light of the setting sun. And my baby boy — no longer a baby — was chasing his best friend through the waves, laughing like the world had never hurt him.

The sight made my eyes sting.

"Thinking about the early trips?" David asked softly, coming to stand beside me.

"Of course," I whispered. "I remember when he couldn't even walk. Now he's almost taller than me."

I lifted my phone and snapped a few photos — trying to catch the motion, the joy. Grace joined us, asking me to send the good ones. Evan stepped up behind me and reached for the phone.

"Let me help. I'll set the timer. We need a group shot."

He took a few — different configurations, a couple candids. He handed the phone back, and I scrolled through the gallery, expecting the usual awkward angles and cut-off heads. Evan had never been the best at candid photography. Kind of ironic for a neurosurgeon.

"You've improved," I said, arching an eyebrow.

"I've practiced," he replied. "I read some stuff about how to frame better. Thought it might help."

The way he said it — like he wanted me to notice, wanted me to *see* that effort — made something in my chest tighten.

He leaned over my shoulder, scrolling with me as we deleted duplicates. And somewhere in the middle of the batch, I noticed it.

A few shots where I wasn't the subject — but he was looking at me anyway.

Not the sunset. Not the kids.

Just me.

And for the first time in years, I let myself wonder what it would feel like... if this was our life.

Maybe it wasn't too late.

24

mackenzie

A frisbee landed near Grace's feet, flung from a group of teens playing nearby. She picked it up without hesitation and tossed it back — clean pass, perfect spin.

David shouted after the kid. "You need someone with a real arm?"

The boy grinned and nodded, and within seconds, David and Grace had joined the boys — ours included — tossing the frisbee around like they were back in college. Grace looked fully recovered. David looked far too pleased with himself.

Evan and I stood watching for a moment, quiet, shoes off, toes curling into the sand. Eventually, we started walking — just the two of us — side by side along the shoreline.

Despite my confusion about our current status — friends, just friends, maybe more — it felt natural to be near him again. Still, I reminded myself that comfort wasn't clarity. Nostalgia and healing could look a lot alike if you didn't check yourself.

I was trying to get to know him again — the Evan who existed now, not the one I once planned to marry.

And then he asked the question.

"This may be out of line," he said gently. "But I've always wondered — did you ever think about having more kids? After Alex?"

I paused, surprised he started there — especially when any talk of children risked reopening the deepest wound we never truly talked about. Our miscarriage was a line we didn't cross, even now.

"I thought about it," I said finally. "But David and I were only together for two years. After that... I didn't want to do it alone. So, Alex is it for me."

A few more quiet steps. Then I asked, "What about you?"

"By the time Gabe came along, things were already unraveling. We didn't want to bring another child into a house that couldn't hold us."

"You and Grace seem... solid now."

He gave a soft laugh. "We worked hard to get here. It wasn't easy. Our marriage was complicated. The divorce, even more. But we made a promise to co-parent with intention. And we've kept that."

"Can I ask... why did you two split?" I asked. "You always look like you get along."

He glanced toward Grace. Then back at me.

"You," he said.

I stopped walking. The breeze stilled around me.

"What?"

He didn't waver. "You were the ghost in our house. Not by name — but in all the things I couldn't let go of. I was still in love with you, Mac. That doesn't just disappear because someone else walks in the room."

I didn't know how to respond. Part of me felt awful. The other part — the one I'd buried — felt hope crackling in my chest.

"That was... years after we'd broken up."

"Not being together doesn't mean I was over you."

My voice was quiet. "That's... a lot."

"In the spirit of fair play," he said, "why did you and David break up?"

"We didn't really *break up*. We met in Vegas. Got married the same day. There was alcohol. Bad decisions."

Evan blinked. "Wait. *You* did that? Married in *one day*?"

I groaned as he started laughing. "Don't sound so surprised."

"I just never pegged you as the impulsive type."

"Well," I said, flushing, "you learn a lot about yourself when you're twenty-something, heartbroken, and three drinks deep."

Talking about that time — about sex, marriage, and another man — with Evan felt strange. Even now. Even at forty.

"Okay," I said. "Maybe we've reached our overshare quota for the day."

Evan's laughter softened. "Fair. I shouldn't have said what I said about you and my marriage. That wasn't fair to you. Or to Grace. I'm sorry."

"Thank you. I appreciate that."

He nodded, and we let the silence stretch for a few beats.

"What do you do for fun these days?" I asked, trying to pivot. "You're not working 80-hour weeks anymore, right?"

"I still work a lot. But yeah — I try to make time for life. I swim, obviously. I've taken up tennis. I'm not great, but it's fun. I'll drive up the coast to little towns, visit wineries. I've learned to scuba dive. And Gabe's been trying to get me into video games."

I blinked. "You? Video games?"

"Don't laugh. I've got a decent KD ratio."

"That I *don't* believe."

He smiled. "We used to talk about doing some of that stuff — road trips, weekends away."

I looked down at my feet. That was a memory I hadn't prepared for.

Evan noticed. He shifted the subject.

"What about your practice? You used to talk about opening your own."

"It didn't work out," I said. "I had Alex by then. David offered to help me start something — financially — but I didn't want to take that from him. I needed to do it on my own."

"You didn't want him to sacrifice for you. That sounds... familiar."

Bad memory number two. I forced a smile.

"I need a minute. Let's head back."

"Of course," he said. "After you."

We turned around. Evan placed a gentle hand on the small of my back. It lingered.

I could feel his thoughts pressing on the edge of silence — same as mine. But neither of us spoke. As we walked back into view, the frisbee game had doubled

— more kids, more laughter, more chaos. But I caught sight of Alex breaking away from the group. He was walking fast. His face was flushed. His eyes locked on us.

On Evan.

He marched right up and stopped in front of us, jaw clenched.

"Did you used to date my mother?"

Evan and I both froze.

Alex looked *straight* at him, unblinking. "You were engaged. I heard my dad say it. Why didn't you tell me? Letting me think you were just some *cool guy*?"

I stepped in. "Alex, sweetheart —"

But he talked over me. "And you, Mom! You're just walking on the beach with him like it's nothing?"

Evan raised both hands. "We didn't know how to explain it. Your mom and I hadn't spoken in years —"

"After your engagement?" Alex snapped. "Did you dump her to marry Dr. Grace?"

"No," we said at the same time.

Grace and David arrived, pulling Alex's attention.

"Dr. Evan and I didn't get married until years after their relationship ended," she said gently. "I know this feels unfair. Adults make decisions that don't always make sense to younger eyes. But I promise — there's more to the story."

"I'm not a kid," Alex muttered. "And I *see* everything. His hand's still on her back."

Evan dropped his hand. Too late.

David was trying — and failing — to hide a smirk. Alex turned to him, indignant.

"Why are you laughing?"

Gabe looked confused. "What's going on? Why's Alex mad?"

The frisbee game dissolved in the background as everyone turned toward us.

"Alex," I said softly. "Come walk with me. Please."

He glared at Evan one last time, then followed me toward the parking lot. David trailed behind us, quiet now. I took a long breath before I started. I needed to be calm — even if my heart was racing.

"Alex, listen to me."

He was pacing, eyes still darting toward Evan.

David spoke up. "Son, I know punching Dr. Evan might feel great right now. *Realmente bueno.*"

I shot David a look.

"Why are you even talking to him?" Alex snapped. "I wish I hadn't come. I wish I hadn't met Gabe."

"No," I said firmly. "Don't go there. None of this is your fault. You didn't do anything wrong. We were going to tell you. We just... didn't know when."

"Are you getting back together?"

I flinched. He was too perceptive. Too fast.

"We're trying to be friends," I said carefully. "Yes, we had a hard breakup. Yes, it was painful. But that was a long time ago. And we've both moved on."

I was lying, but it was the safest version of the truth I could offer him right now.

David, ever the instigator, chimed in. "If they *were* getting back together — would that be a problem?"

Alex shrugged, then scowled. "I don't know. I don't *know* him."

"You're allowed to feel that way," David said gently. "It's okay not to know how to feel."

"Did you know he was going to be here?" Alex asked suddenly. "Is that why you picked this place?"

"No," I said quickly. "I had no idea. None. I would *never* put you in that position on purpose."

He studied my face for a long moment. "I believe you. But... I needed to ask."

I pulled him into a hug. He leaned into it — just for a second — before stepping back.

"I'll try to be nice to him. For you."

He kissed my cheek, shoved his hands into his pockets, and wandered back toward the waves.

David looked over at me. "I know you don't want to hear this, but I'm proud of him. He stood his ground. Didn't back down. *Es el duro.*"

"You're proud of him for trying to fight a grown man?"

David grinned. "It's a man thing. He's protecting the people he loves. That's growth."

I didn't love that version of growth. Growing up was overrated.

We walked back to where the others waited. Gabe was standing near Alex again, throwing rocks into the surf. Evan glanced up as we approached.

"Should I run?" he asked.

"Maybe," I said, raising an eyebrow. "Might be safer."

Grace chuckled behind her hand.

I looked out at my son — standing between the waves and the setting sun, caught halfway between boyhood and something bigger.

And I realized something I hadn't wanted to admit.

We were all growing up.

Whether we wanted to or not.

25

evan

I'd been feeling pretty good about the direction things were heading — until Alex stormed up and demanded answers.

I couldn't even blame him. If I were thirteen and overheard something like that about my mom, I'd react the same way. Maybe Grace and I should've said something to Gabe sooner — but what do you even say when *you* don't know what this is yet?

After the commotion died down and the Stephens crew walked away, Grace and I stayed on the beach, both of us quiet for a minute. The waves rolled in. The boys tossed a frisbee. Mac and David were still talking to Alex in the distance.

Finally, Grace sighed. "We need to talk to him."

I knew who she meant. "Yeah. I've been thinking the same thing."

"We can't let Gabe find out what's happening through whispers or teen gossip. Especially not when he already struggles with change. This kind of stuff — it *unlocks* him, Evan."

I nodded, because she was right. Gabe didn't handle sudden shifts well. New schedules, unfamiliar faces, even transitions between games and meals — they could throw him off completely. He liked patterns. Predictability. Surprises made him feel unsafe.

"We tell him when we *know* something," I said. "Not when we're still trying to figure it out ourselves."

She folded her arms. "Exactly. I know how you feel about Mac. And I'm not here to block anything — but I'm asking you to think long-term. If it's serious, we'll adjust. But if it's just nostalgia or a moment—"

"It's not," I said quickly. "It's not a moment."

She gave me a look. Not disbelieving — just cautious. Protective. Like a mom should be.

I took a deep breath. "But I hear you. I don't want Gabe thrown into anything messy. If this *is* something real, I'll make sure he knows I'm still his constant. Nothing about how I show up for him changes."

Grace's shoulders softened, just a little. "Good. Because that's what he needs. He needs anchors. Not chaos. Not instability. Especially not from the people he trusts the most."

I looked out at Gabe, now laughing as he chased the frisbee with the other boys, and felt a pang in my chest. "He comes first."

"Always," she agreed.

We stood side by side, not touching, not talking, just watching our son. And for a moment, it felt like the old days — back when we didn't have all these complications, just two people trying to raise a good kid the best way we knew how.

She nudged my arm. "You think we should tell him soon?"

"When we're sure," I said. "Not before."

She nodded. "Fair."

And just like that, we were back on the same page.

Then she glanced down and said, "With all that going on, I forgot to tell you — David wants to take us to Little Havana tomorrow. No swim sessions during the day, and the food's supposed to be great. Music, shops, coffee. A real day off."

I nodded slowly. "Sounds good. I've never been."

"Don't know if Mac knows. David might've said something. I'll check in with her."

I didn't press. Grace had already given me more grace than I probably deserved.

About ten minutes later, I saw Mac, David, and Alex walking back toward us. Alex had clearly cooled off. He passed by without a word — just headed straight for the shoreline, where Gabe left the group to join him.

They'd talk. Probably about how ridiculous we were. Teen judgment was the one certainty in life.

Mac and David lingered behind. She gave me a half-smile. "Sorry about that. He's usually more... restrained."

Grace, now fully herself again, spoke up. "I'd be *disappointed* if he didn't try to defend his mom. I'd hope Gabe would do the same for me."

She reached for David's hand and pulled him toward the boys.

I turned to Mac. "So... your son threatened to jump me."

She didn't look remotely sorry. "I *said* I was sorry."

I laughed. "He had me genuinely thinking through my options. I didn't want to get knocked out by a middle schooler."

I looked at her then — *really* looked. And before I knew it, I'd stepped closer. "He's exactly what I'd imagine your son would be. Feisty. Loyal."

Her breath caught — just slightly. She looked up at me. "And without all the baggage I grew up with. Sometimes I look at him and wonder — is that who I could've been, if my dad had lived?"

I reached up, instinctively brushing her cheek with my hand. Her eyes closed as I touched her.

"You had a hard path," I said gently. "But look what you've done with it. You became a doctor. You raised a phenomenal kid. You carved out a life on your terms."

"I know," she whispered. "But it still wasn't the life I thought I'd have."

A pause. Her voice was softer now. "Sometimes I think about us — and I wonder, if we crumbled so easily from one match result and a few miles apart... could we have really made it?"

I didn't hesitate. "If we'd matched in the same city? Same hospital? We'd still be together."

"But then we wouldn't have our sons."

"I think about that too," I admitted. "But I still believe we were meant to be. Maybe we still are."

That stopped her.

She blinked — once — and then stepped back, retreating into familiar armor.

"Oh my," she said, glancing down at her wrist like there was a watch there. "Look at the time. We've got to get the boys back. Early morning tomorrow."

And just like that, the moment passed.

She walked away before I could say anything else. I didn't follow.

Maybe she needed space. Maybe I did too.

I'd let Grace tell her about Little Havana.

On the ride back, the boys were quiet — which made me nervous at first. But when I turned to check on them, both were out cold in the backseat.

That helped. A little.

David glanced at them through the mirror. "Well... at least we're not getting ambushed again tonight."

Grace laughed. "Still, we should talk to Gabe. I don't want Alex's anger to become Gabe's confusion."

Mac nodded. "I agree. I can talk to both boys later if that helps. I just want everyone to be comfortable. I don't want them to feel like they *can't* ask questions."

Grace turned toward the front. "We'll talk to Gabe first, and we'll loop in the boys when it feels right."

David shifted gears. "So. Little Havana tomorrow?"

"I didn't know that was the plan," Mac said, casting a glance in my direction.

I looked down, sheepish. I'd meant to tell her — then I got distracted. Then... I chickened out.

She let the silence hang for just long enough before adding, "But I'd love to go. It's been a while. Should be fun."

She didn't smile — not fully. But she didn't shut me out either.

I took that as a small win.

Here's hoping tomorrow goes better than tonight did.

26

david

The ride back from Miami Beach was quiet in the back seat — which meant it was finally safe to speak. I glanced in the rearview mirror and saw that Mac and Evan were leaned back, eyes closed, caught somewhere between post-beach exhaustion and whatever tension still lingered from earlier.

I glanced over at Grace. She had her head leaned against the window, but I could tell her mind was spinning. She looked like someone holding her breath, waiting for the secondhand sting of something she already chose to walk away from. That kind of ache? You don't show it, but it shows anyway.

She must've felt me looking. "What?" she asked, not even turning.

"Can I ask you something?"

Grace sighed but nodded. "Shoot."

"Why are you doing this? Helping Evan get back with Mac, I mean."

She turned to me then, slow and deliberate. "You ever love somebody who didn't love you the same way? Or maybe they did — but they loved someone else just a little more?"

I didn't answer.

Grace gave a tired half-shrug. "That's what it was like. When Evan and I got married, it felt right. Safe. He was grieving his dad, I was trying to keep both our heads above water. And when it started, I think we really were just friends who didn't want to be alone."

I stayed quiet. Not out of judgment — just because I knew exactly what she meant.

"I ignored the signs," she said. "Thought maybe I could love him enough for the both of us. But that only works until you wake up and realize you're the only one carrying the damn thing."

I nodded slowly. "That's real."

"Therapy helped," she said. "Now I just want peace. For him, for me, for Gabe most of all."

"That's not sappy," I said. "That's love — just not the kind that's easy."

Grace looked out the window again. "And you? You're real gung-ho about getting Mac back with Evan too."

I chuckled low in my throat. "Let's just say the romantic part of my relationship with Mac ended a long time ago. We were two kids who got drunk in Vegas and tried to parent our way into being soulmates. Turns out, co-parenting we're great at. Being married? Not so much."

Grace cracked a smile. "Of course y'all got married in Vegas. Y'all give chaos couple energy."

I put a hand to my chest, mock offended. "And yet I take that with pride."

She laughed. "You're a mess."

"Maybe," I said. "But I want her happy. That's it. And if this"—I gestured toward the two knocked-out passengers in the second row—"is her happy? Then I'll do my part."

Grace leaned her head back and smiled softly. "You ever think we're the grown-ups here?"

"Oh, 100 percent. They're still in act one of their soap opera."

She laughed again, but the mood shifted just slightly. She was still holding something close to the chest. I let it be. Some stories aren't meant to be told all at once.

Instead, I pivoted. "So. Havana."

Grace perked up. "Still planning on dancing?"

"Absolutely. They've got a club down there with a live band. You bring the shoes, I'll bring the moves."

She raised an eyebrow. "Can Mac dance?"

"Not when I met her," I said, grinning. "But she's improved."

"Evan's alright," she added. "Little stiff, but he's got rhythm."

"And the boys?" I asked.

"We'll cross that bridge if they show up."

Just then, there was a tap on my shoulder.

"You two have been whispering the whole ride," Mac said from the back seat. "Are you talking about us?"

Her tone was teasing, but her eyes said she was half-serious.

Grace didn't skip a beat. "Wouldn't you like to know?"

Evan stirred behind her. "I would, actually."

I looked over at Grace. Busted. Our top-secret mission wasn't so top-secret after all.

When Mac leaned back again, Grace whispered, "You still down for Operation Amor?"

"I already bought the tickets," I replied. "They won't even see it coming."

"We don't have much time," she said. "If this doesn't work…"

"It will," I said. "Or we go out swingin'."

27

mackenzie

Back at the hotel, I tried not to drown in my own thoughts — but it wasn't easy. Everything felt like too much.

First, my son was upset with me.

When David and I walked Alex to his dorm, we tried again to talk about what had happened. But all he said was that he needed time to think. We told him we'd check in tomorrow night after the Little Havana trip — the trip I apparently had no say in attending.

I was still a little annoyed about that, by the way. Grace just *informed* me we were going. Like it was no big deal. Like this was just a casual outing with "a friend."

Healing, my ass.

Everything felt like it was spinning out of control. I sat in silence on the ride back, fuming quietly as David drove, knowing full well he and Grace had been talking about me. I couldn't catch the full conversation, but I didn't need to. My life was apparently the subject of some matchmaker conspiracy, and I was just along for the ride.

My head was full. My heart was heavy. And I hadn't been swimming in two days.

That, at least, I could fix.

Still wearing my blue swimsuit and a coverup, I dug around in my luggage for my swim cap and grabbed a towel. A few laps in the hotel pool sounded like the only thing that could help me shake the day off. I made my way down to the first floor, bypassed the front desk, and walked straight into the glowing, humid pool room.

As expected, I wasn't alone.

A couple had claimed a corner of the pool for themselves — definitely making out, *hopefully* not doing anything else. They looked up, annoyed, when I opened the door.

"Hello," I said casually.

"Oh! Sorry — we didn't think anyone would be down here this late," the girl said, flustered.

Her boyfriend just grunted. Real welcoming.

"I just need to get a few laps in. I'll stay out of your way," I told them.

"Oh. Enjoy your swim!" she replied quickly. He grunted again. She elbowed him. A mumbled "hey" followed. I rolled my eyes and assessed the pool layout, calculating the best path that wouldn't bring me too close to their little love nest.

I pulled off my coverup and eased myself into the water. I've never been the diving type. Not since Gulf Shores. The idea of being swallowed by water in a single plunge still makes my chest tighten. So I slip in slow, always.

Fifteen laps later — short pool, but it still counted — I finally felt something close to peace. The couple had left. Maybe I had unintentionally cockblocked them. Oh well.

Stepping out of the water, I felt steadier. Clearer. And honestly? A little pissed at myself.

All this chaos in my head? It wasn't Evan's fault. He hadn't done anything wrong. But I'd let myself drift. I'd lost my routine. Got caught in memories.

The past was sweet, but it was also over. We were different now — older, more complicated, with new priorities. I couldn't keep living like I was back in college. I needed to get back to the version of me I actually liked. The one I built after it all fell apart.

I thought about calling Ree again, but I didn't have it in me to talk. I needed quiet. Stillness. Reflection.

Back in my room, I grabbed my shower stuff and stood under the stream for longer than usual. Hot water always helps. Helps me think. Helps me forget.

When I reached for the body wash, I paused. The label caught me off guard. It was the scent my momma used when I was little. The original formula — harder to find now. I took a breath and let it hit me.

It smelled like childhood.

Like my daddy, my momma, my brother, and my grandma. Like good times — the few we had before things got hard. Before people started dying and blaming and leaving.

A lump caught in my throat. I didn't cry. Not quite. But I felt it.

I've never told many people the full story. Not even David when we were married. Evan, though... I told him everything. Every jagged, ugly truth.

My dad's death. How no one ever said it out loud, but they treated me like it was my fault. The way my mom looked at me. The way my brother never came back around. How after Momma died, my grandma made sure I never forgot how much they thought I owed.

Like I had to *atone* for living.

But Evan never bought into that. When I finally told him, he didn't flinch. He didn't ask questions. He just held me. That hug — it made me feel like I wasn't broken. Like maybe I didn't deserve to carry all that shame.

That's why it hurt so much when he didn't believe me. When the internship stuff happened and he didn't stand by me — that broke something I didn't know was still fragile.

By the time I got out of the shower, I was exhausted. I did my skincare and hair routine and crawled into bed, ready to forget the world.

But of course, the world didn't forget me.

Ree

> Hey girl. Just checking in. How are things going with you and Evan? And how is Alex doing at the Academy? If you want to talk, call me!

I smiled. I loved her for reaching out, but I couldn't do it tonight. I'd be up for hours rehashing everything. I'd call her tomorrow.

Then another ding.

Evan

Mac.

I heard the song 'Outstanding' right before I got in bed.

I thought of you.

My breath caught.

That song. After his sister's wedding, he'd whisper-sing it to me when we were alone. Said it reminded him of how "amazing" I was. Of how I was his choice.

I sat up, heart thudding.

Was this just nostalgia? Or was it something deeper?

I didn't know yet. But I was going to find out.

Tomorrow.

28

mackenzie

Tuesday morning, I woke up with something I hadn't felt in a few days: clarity.

Last night's swim had reset me — cleared the mental fog, steadied my nerves, and helped me feel like myself again. Not the confused woman overthinking every decision. Not the mom second-guessing every conversation. Just... *me.*

And the truth? I'm still in love with Evan.

I've known it. Quietly. For years. But last night, I finally admitted it — to myself, out loud, no qualifiers. I didn't know if anything would come of it or even if it *should.* But I wasn't hiding from it anymore.

Fifteen years ago, I didn't have this voice. This strength. If I had, maybe things with Evan would've turned out differently. Maybe we would've stayed together. Built the life we once dreamed of.

But we didn't.

And I can't undo that.

What I can do is move forward from here.

As I rolled over in bed, my phone buzzed with a message from Grace.

> Leaving in 20 minutes. Meet in the lobby.

> WE WILL LEAVE YOU!

Right. Little Havana. That was today.

I threw back the covers and got moving. A quick wash-up, a generous coat of sunscreen, and I slipped into a turquoise sundress with white Chucks. I piled my braids into a high bun, grabbed my day bag, and double-checked for sunglasses and cash.

As I rushed out the door, I texted Alex and Gabe in our group chat. Both boys were heading to the Academy early this morning for swim conditioning. They'd eat breakfast with the other recruits and **maybe** meet up with us later in the afternoon. Alex had asked for space last night, and I wanted to honor that. Gabe, from what Evan said, was still feeling things out — but agreed to meet us later for a possible dinner after training wrapped.

Still, the parent in me didn't love the idea of not seeing either of them in person before we left. They were only 12 and 13. But both Evan and I had been assured that this morning was structured and supervised — and that we'd be checking in again later this evening. I made a mental note to ask Evan what the daily schedule looked like for the rest of the week.

By the time I got downstairs, Grace was already waiting in the lobby, tapping her foot like she was ready to walk off without me.

"Girl, were you alone last night? I called and left a text. You sleep like the dead," she said, hands on hips.

I held up my phone with an apologetic smile. "I swear I didn't see it. I went for a swim late last night — needed to clear my head."

Grace perked up. "Ooooh. And did you meet anyone while clearing said head?"

I shook my head with a laugh. "No sexy pool rendezvous. Just me, a couple making out in the corner, and my thoughts. Though I might have ruined their little late-night plans."

"That's a shame. Because I could really use someone's fun, slightly scandalous story right now. I'm in a dry spell so long I think I'm legally a desert."

"You told me you had a boyfriend," I teased.

"I said I was seeing someone. Not the same thing." Grace rolled her eyes. "It's complicated. I don't even know if he knows I'm out of town."

I gave her a look. "You're gorgeous. How does he not know that?"

"California men," she sighed. "Different breed. And remember, I've made some terrible choices with men. You and I might need to form a support group."

"We'd call it 'Women Who Should Know Better.' I'll be the treasurer," I said, slinging my bag over my shoulder. "Anyway — where are the guys?"

"Late," she said with a groan. "Slower than both of us, somehow."

"Can we leave them?" I half-joked.

Grace had just started dialing a number when the hotel doors opened and both men walked in — David, fresh-faced and grinning, and Evan, looking entirely too comfortable for someone who'd nearly blown up my whole emotional state less than 24 hours ago.

I raised a brow. "David, don't you have a room here?"

He shrugged. "I picked Evan up this morning. We were going to sneak over to the Academy, check in on the boys."

"You were going to see them without us?" I asked, a little sharper than I intended.

David held up his hands. "We thought a quick one-on-one — man to man — might help smooth things over. Nothing secretive, I promise."

Evan added, "Didn't work anyway. They were already at the pool when we got there. Morning swim practice."

"Good," I said, softening. "They need the structure."

"Speaking of structure," Evan said, "we got into a debate on the way back. Basketball versus swimming. Who's the better athlete."

"Oh no." I shook my head. "Don't tell me y'all are planning some kind of father-dad biathlon?"

"We might," David grinned. "Could be fun."

I turned to Evan. "You do know David swam in college, right?"

Evan looked betrayed. "That's not what he told me. Said he was out of shape."

"Did I lie?" David said, smirking. "I'm older now. Doesn't mean I don't have muscle memory."

We all laughed, even Evan — who was already plotting revenge, I could tell.

"Fine," Evan said, dramatically. "I won't be fooled again."

He sang the line like he was on CSI: Miami, and Grace and I groaned in unison.

"No. Absolutely not," Grace said. "Leave the dad jokes in the Tahoe."

"That's where we're headed," David said. "Mac, your Tahoe's already in valet. Let's hit La Colada for coffee and get this day started."

And just like that, we were off — four adults, two missing kids, one chaotic past, and a whole lot of unresolved feelings. But for the first time in a while, I felt ready to handle it.

29

evan

The conversation about having more children started off light — until it didn't.

Grace and David had been laughing and giggling about how ironic it was for us to have had our first child around the same time as one another, when I saw the look spread across Mac's face.

There had almost been a child before Alex — at least that's what we thought during our third year of med school when she was two weeks late.

I remember that month like it was yesterday. I was on my trauma surgery sub-specialty rotation, and Mac was doing general surgery. Most nights, we barely saw each other — unless we were lucky enough to be on-call at the same time. And when we were? We made the most of it.

We had our spot. One call room we always managed to slip into when we needed five minutes — or when adrenaline was high enough to ignore the exhaustion. And that month, we were reckless.

We didn't think about the fact that we'd both caught a stomach bug. We didn't think about whether the antibiotics or the vomiting had impacted her birth control. We were too damn tired, too wound up, and too in love.

But we thought about it later.

She took the test when she still hadn't started. Positive.

We panicked. Talked about names. Residency schedules. Rotations. We built a life in our heads over the span of two days. And then her period came.

I didn't know I would grieve that. Neither of us wanted a baby back then. But in those two days, it stopped being a scare. It became a maybe.

A what-if.

And I guess I never fully put that memory away.

But I pushed it aside now. Today was about the present. About time with Mac. About the fact that we were here — in Miami — together. And I wasn't going to waste a single second of it.

"Evan, where are you?"

Grace's voice pulled me back. I looked up to see her eyeing me from across the van.

"Yeah, sorry. Just thinking," I said, glancing at Mac beside me. Our eyes met — hers were guarded — and then she looked away.

"What do you need, Dr. Grace? Are we almost there?"

"Almost. So, are we stopping at La Colada Gourmet? Isn't that what you said, David?"

David grinned. "Some of the best Cuban coffee around. I brought my mother here once — she talked about it for months. And we've got family in Cuba. We know Cuban coffee."

I frowned. "I thought you were from Spain?"

"My mother is. But her cousins and siblings are scattered — Cuba, Brazil, Mexico. It's a big family. I'm the slacker for only having one kid."

He shot a look at Mac.

She rolled her eyes and slapped his arm. "Don't drag me into that!"

"My mother does too," he said, laughing. "We're here!"

The coffee shop was small — only a few parking spaces out front. David dropped us off to find a spot.

Inside, we ordered our drinks. Cuban espresso for me and Grace. A cortado for David. A pastry sampler for the table. Mac ordered her usual and looked surprisingly comfortable — like this was a familiar ritual.

David found a spot quicker than expected and slid into the booth just as his drink arrived.

"I've missed this," he said, holding up his cup. "I've been ordering their beans for years. Still never tastes the same at home."

Mac smirked. "Must be the water."

"What's the tour plan?" I asked.

Grace pulled out her phone. "Little Havana Food & Cultural Tour. We'll walk, eat, and learn. It starts at 11, so we've got time."

"Is there parking at the theater?"

"Limited," David said. "If I have to park far next time, y'all are walking too."

After finishing our drinks, we headed to the historic Tower Theater and joined the tour group. Five others were already gathered — two couples and one solo traveler. The lobby was full of vibrant posters and a featured exhibit on Celia Cruz. While we waited, I wandered toward the display, letting the rhythm of the city seep in.

Our guide, Leo, appeared shortly after. Latino, mid-40s, with a warm voice and sharp energy. He welcomed us and launched into a quick history of the theater before leading us out onto Calle Ocho.

Our first stop? The Ball & Chain.

Grace gasped when she saw the memo board. "It's BachaTuesday!" she said, doing a little shimmy. "We're coming back tonight!"

The group moved ahead. I lingered with Mac.

"You watching us dance tonight?" I teased. "Still not a fan of the spotlight?"

She turned toward me, eyelashes fluttering playfully. "It's been a while since you saw me dance."

I raised a brow. "Because you refused to dance in public."

"That was then. This is now." She curtsied. "I bet I'll outdance you."

"You're on. What's the wager?"

"I'll let you know later. Just remember — you don't know me like you used to." She winked and walked ahead.

I followed, watching her go — damn, she was right. I didn't know this version of her. But I wanted to.

We stopped at Cubaocho Museum next — part gallery, part performance space. Grace and David lingered toward the back, giving us space. Subtle, but intentional.

Mac pointed to a mural on the wall across the street. "I love murals. The detail, the scale, the effort... I admire it. Even when it's stories off the ground."

"You could take an art class."

She snorted. "Do you not remember me failing the brain diagram assignment in anatomy? Dr. Martinelli only passed me because I described it all verbally."

"Oh, I remember. He told me your drawing looked like a squashed squid."

"And he wasn't wrong." She paused, then pointed toward a sculpture fountain. "Maybe I should try sculpting instead."

"With Play-Doh?"

"Exactly."

I laughed. "Not Da Vinci, huh?"

"Not even close."

The next stop was Havana Classic Cigars. Leo gave a quick demo on rolling and the cultural significance. Mac stood close, listening intently. Grace elbowed me with a knowing grin.

"I see you two are speaking more."

"And?" I elbowed her back. "Pay attention to the cigars, Dr. Grace."

After the demo, we each bought a cigar.

"I don't even want to smoke it," Mac said, sticking hers between her teeth. "It just makes me feel sexy and powerful."

David snorted. "You're not a smoker."

"True. I choked on secondhand weed in college."

"Exactly."

Grace grabbed her phone. "Wait — photo op! Mac, Evan, pose!"

Mac slipped her arm around my waist without hesitation. I felt her settle into me — easy, natural. We both lifted our cigars for the camera.

Click.

"I need that picture," Mac said.

"Later. Tour's moving," Grace replied, disappearing with David.

I held Mac back for a second.

"I'm glad we ran into each other again," I said. "I forgot how much I missed you."

She blinked, then kissed my cheek. "I've missed you too."

We caught up at Domino Park — tables lined with locals slamming dominos and talking trash. I could've stayed all day.

"Do you play?" I asked.

"I used to. Back when I was five, playing with my parents and my grand-mother on weekends. Alex knows how — picked it up during swim meets."

"You think I can take him?"

"Only one way to find out."

I nodded. "So... should I get to know your son better?"

"Maybe," she said softly. "We'll see how today goes."

We talked sports, family, old inside jokes. She remembered I liked cricket — and I remembered everything about her, even the things I'd tried to forget.

At the next stop, Grace handed us guava pastelitos. Mac took one bite and moaned.

"God, that's good. When's lunch?"

I was thinking the same thing — about the pastry, and her.

"We've got a few stops left."

"Or," she said, "we ditch the tour."

My heart skipped.

"You sure? Where do you want to go?"

She nodded. "With you? Anywhere."

I texted Grace and shoved my phone in my pocket.

"Alright," I said, holding out my hand. Mac laced her fingers with mine instantly. "Lead the way."

30

grace

David and I had just reached the next stop on the tour when Evan's text came through.

David read it over my shoulder and grinned. "Well, look at that. Sounds like somebody's finally making a move."

I smiled, but I didn't get ahead of myself. "Let's not pop the champagne just yet. But it's a good sign. If they can go a whole afternoon without falling into an argument or overanalyzing everything, we might actually be onto something."

David snorted. "You know, the best part of this whole trip might be getting out of the matchmaking business once we hit Key West. They're not stupid. They know what we're doing."

"Of course they know. We've been about as subtle as a bullhorn. But I think they're finally starting to want this for themselves. That's the difference."

"Agreed. And just for the record, I've got all the tickets — four to Key West tomorrow morning, and return trips for us that night. Their return's scheduled for Thursday."

I gave him a nod. "And the surprise at the hotel?"

"Handled. They'll be impressed. If they make it there without imploding."

That made me laugh. "We should be so lucky."

David studied me a little more seriously then. "You doing okay?"

I paused. The question wasn't unexpected, but the softness in his tone threw me for a second.

"Yeah," I said. "This trip's been good. Weirdly healing, in some ways. But also... it brings up things. You know?"

"I do."

"I started all this because I wanted Evan to have something good again. But I guess I didn't think too hard about what it would feel like to watch someone I love — someone I helped repair — fall back in love with the person who broke him."

David didn't jump in with a pep talk. He just nodded, quiet.

"But tonight," I continued, "I'm looking forward to the dancing. I don't know a damn thing about bachata, but I plan on pretending I do."

"Do I get the honor of being your partner?" he asked, half-playful, half-sincere.

I gave him a look. "Thank you for the offer, but no. No windows opened that I don't intend to walk through."

He laughed. "Was that a metaphor or a proverb?"

"Probably both. Either way, I meant it."

He raised both hands in mock surrender. "Fair enough. I'll just have to find someone else to embarrass on the dance floor. Hopefully someone single."

"You won't have a problem."

And with that, we rejoined the group, just two friends walking the line between past and present hoping our favorite couple could do the same.

31

mackenzie

We bailed on the tour the second it ended and started walking, stomachs growling. I had been craving a Cuban sandwich all morning, but the ten-block walk to Sanguich de Miami was a no-go. Not in this heat. We settled on a Thai tapas spot around the corner — street food-style, close enough to comfort.

Once we gave our name to the hostess, we stepped aside to wait. And instinctively, we each put some space between us.

It was subtle, but I noticed.

I needed the distance. We'd spent all morning touching — hands, shoulders, arms brushing — and every small connection was pulling me back in. Back to a place I thought I'd buried years ago.

I wasn't in my twenties anymore. This wasn't some summer fling.

And yet... here we were. Still able to talk. Still able to laugh. Still drawn to each other in that quiet, electric way that had always been there. Only now, we had lived entire lives apart. We were different — but not as different as I expected.

There were a few ways this could go. We could pretend this trip was just about the kids and the past. Or we could give in to the attraction and enjoy whatever it was, however long it lasted.

But then what?

Losing him once broke me.

Evan turned toward me. "I've got to ask — David? I didn't think you two would even get along."

"Honestly, we get along fine now. But we were never really a couple. He was more interested in being a dad than a husband, and I wasn't in love with him. We both knew it. We just didn't say it out loud until the damage was done."

Evan nodded slowly. "I get it. Grace and I... we worked a few cases together. Grew close. She convinced me we could make it work, even if I wasn't fully in it."

"You said I was the reason it ended," I said quietly. "What did you mean by that?"

He hesitated. "I never stopped being in love with you. I knew it before I married her. I just didn't want to admit it. After you and I ended, and with everything else happening — my dad dying, work piling up — I thought a relationship without all the emotion would be easier to maintain."

I swallowed. Hard.

Even if I hadn't been part of their story, hearing that still landed like a gut punch.

"I wasn't there, but... I'm sorry," I said.

"You don't need to be. That wasn't your fault." He glanced away for a second, then back. "But let's save the heavy stuff for another time."

He gave me a lifeline, and I took it. "When did you start teaching Gabe to swim?"

"Pretty early. I kept swimming after we split. My therapist encouraged it. Gabe just took to the water like he was born for it."

Our name was called then. Saved by spring rolls.

The second we stepped into the restaurant, the smells hit me like a full-body hug — spicy, rich, aromatic. It wasn't just the food making my senses come alive, though. It was everything. The closeness. His voice. The quiet look he gave me when he thought I wasn't paying attention.

We sat across from each other and ordered — spring rolls, green curry, pad Thai. Shrimp in everything. I gripped my water glass tighter than necessary, just to keep my hands from doing anything they shouldn't.

"So how's Liza? Is she still with Stephon?" I asked, redirecting.

"She's doing great. They just had a baby — a girl — about a month ago. Surprise pregnancy after years of trying."

"That's amazing. And Joe?"

"Married. Two daughters. Living out in San Diego, doing radiology."

"So you're the only one with a son?"

Evan chuckled. "Yep. Gabe's bitter about it, too. He keeps saying he needs a brother or a boy cousin. Thinks he's the odd one out."

We both laughed, then went quiet. The implication hung in the air like steam from the curry.

"Gabe must be desperate," I said, trying to shake it off. "He just likes Alex. They get along well. He doesn't know me that well. Or Alex." I took another sip of water. "Oh god, I'm rambling."

"You're fine," Evan said, softly.

But I didn't feel fine. I was spinning — jumping topics, clinging to safe conversation.

I talked about Alex. About swimming. About how he reminded me of Evan.

Evan didn't interrupt. Just listened, like he always had.

"I still have contacts in the swim world," he said. "If this place doesn't work out, or you want other options, I've got you."

"Thanks. Really. He wants the Olympics one day. When we talk about it... I always think of you."

Evan reached across the table and took my hand.

"You could've called," he said. "Anytime. I would've picked up. I always would've picked up for you."

I froze. My heart lodged somewhere between my throat and my stomach.

Then the food arrived, and I didn't have to respond.

We ate like we hadn't eaten in days, and when we finally stumbled out of the restaurant, I leaned back against the warm brick wall and stretched.

"God, that was good. I need a nap."

My skirt rode up as I stretched, and I felt Evan's eyes on me. I didn't rush to fix it. I let it linger, just for a second, before tugging it back down.

I didn't know who I was trying to convince anymore — him or me.

Then his phone rang. Grace, of course.

"You two done chatting?" she asked. "We're starving."

"We just finished at Thai Tapas," Evan replied.

Grace gasped theatrically. "You ate without us? Wow. So rude."

"Sorry," Evan said, not sounding sorry at all. "We'll catch up with you later."

He hung up and looked at me. "We'll pay for that later. You wanna walk?"

I nodded. Words weren't safe anymore.

We ended up at Domino Park, and Evan — trying to earn some kind of cultural credibility — decided to join a game. We found a table with a teenage player named Diego, who let Evan sit in after a quick loss from his previous opponent.

I tried to cheer Evan on, but I leaned over his shoulder a little too closely. Might've thrown off his game. Okay — definitely threw off his game.

Diego grinned at me as he slammed down his final piece. "You're gonna be good at this one day — but not if she's hanging on you like that. You gotta concentrate, man!"

Evan laughed. "Noted."

Diego looked at me. "But I get it. I'd be distracted too."

We walked off with Evan grinning like a fool.

"So," he said, nudging me with his shoulder. "Do I still get to keep my Black card?"

"You held your own," I said, bumping him back. "But let's see what you do tonight at the Ball and Chain. If you can dance, we'll talk."

We locked eyes.

And right there, on a quiet street in Little Havana, I knew.

I was going to let it happen.

Whatever this thing was — whatever step came next — I was done fighting it.

I reached for his hand. He laced his fingers through mine like he'd never let go.

"Outstanding," he said.

And for once, I believed him.

32

mackenzie

I asked Evan if he wanted to play another game, but he shook his head. "I want to sit for a bit," he said.

We found a small patch of grass just off the path—still close enough to hear the clatter of dominoes, but far enough to focus on each other.

"So... you want to know about my life now?" I asked, settling cross-legged on the grass.

Evan sat close beside me — close enough to feel the warmth radiating between us. "Yeah. What do you do for fun? I still can't believe you stayed in Tennessee."

"I probably wouldn't have, if I hadn't gotten pregnant." I tucked a loose braid back into my bun. "The residency program worked with me so I could finish on time, then offered me a job. They made it easy to be a doctor and a mom — so I stayed. These days, fun looks like getting Alex to swim practice on time and dancing with my friends once a month, if I'm lucky." I smiled. "And yes, I dance in public now. Growth."

Evan raised a brow. "And me staying in San Francisco?"

"Ironic, but I kind of owe that to you. Reporting the nurse — the one whose name shall not be spoken — it gave me a lot of respect. I ended up as chief resident, then they offered me a faculty role. By then, Grace and I were expecting Gabe... so I stayed." He held up a finger, grinning. "Wait. How much dancing have you been doing?"

"Occasional. Calm down." I smirked. "And I'm glad something good came from San Fran. That mess doesn't hurt the same anymore. Funny how healing works."

Evan stretched his legs out in front of him — those long, lean swimmer legs — and I laid back in the grass beside him. My bag became a makeshift pillow, and I let my eyes drift upward. The sky was a bold, cloud-swirled blue.

I couldn't remember the last time I let myself just lie still and watch the sky.

The sounds around us faded — voices, traffic, breeze — all muffled by how aware I was of him. His breathing. His presence. The slow, featherlight way his fingers brushed the side of my neck.

He was drawing circles just below my ear — tracing a path that made my whole body lean into his touch.

"This feels like déjà vu," he murmured. "A sunny day on the lawn, taking a break. Relaxing together."

I let my eyes close, giving in to the feel of his hand sliding lower — across my collarbone, between my breasts, skimming down to my belly. His palm stopped at the curve of my hips, fingertips hovering over the vee of my thighs. He was close — dangerously close — and every nerve in my body responded.

He whispered, "Do you want me to stop?"

Instead of answering, I hitched my dress up — slow and deliberate.

Evan leaned closer. "I remember every curve of you..."

His hand glided down my thigh, wrapping fabric around his fingers, inching up...

"What you like..."

I swallowed a sound.

"How long it takes..."

He was watching me — not just my body, but my face — trying to gauge how far I'd let him go. And whether he should keep going.

I wasn't twenty anymore. And this wasn't a dorm room with the door barely locked.

I sat up suddenly, breath catching. "Not here," I whispered, standing too fast and nearly tripping over my own feet.

Evan caught me. "Whoa. Be careful."

"I'm fine," I muttered. "But I wouldn't be falling if you hadn't tried me a minute ago."

He grinned. "You've been feeling it too — the pull. Even after all these years. And you know I love watching you... I always did."

I rolled my eyes, but I was blushing. He wasn't wrong.

"How far were you planning to take that?" I asked as casually as I could, even as my body was still catching up.

He didn't answer. His phone chimed.

Grace. Of course.

"What have you two been up to?" she teased when Evan answered. "Actually — never mind. I don't wanna know."

"David's been collecting numbers," she added. "Including one from a woman on the tour. I hope her husband—"

"Boyfriend!" David called in the background. "I don't mess with married women!"

"He better not be packing," Grace muttered. "And if he is, he better have good aim. I'm not getting shot over your need for a different ass every night."

"Women want to tame me," David said with zero shame.

"You two are like Frick and Frack," Evan said, laughing.

I checked my watch. "We've been in the park for hours."

"Let's eat," David suggested. "I heard Café La Trova is nearby."

We agreed and met them there. The bar was gorgeous, the kind of place that felt alive — warm wood, Cuban jazz, bright cocktails.

Everyone ordered a drink except David, who said he needed to stay sober for dancing. He claimed he'd embarrass us all if he got drunk and tried to salsa.

Dinner was amazing — sharp flavors, smooth rum, easy laughter. Grace kept trying to get me to spill about the afternoon, but I kept my mouth shut.

That didn't stop her.

"Let's see... you played dominoes and dethroned that old man from this morning? Took a nap in the park? Had sex in the park? Hit up a one-hour motel?"

"David already told me you went shopping while he tried to pick up anything with a pulse. I warned you about him," I said, grinning. "Handsome or not — he's not worth the drama."

Grace let out a dramatic sigh.

"I know you people are talking about me," David said flatly.

We skipped dessert and walked down to Azucar Ice Cream.

The flavors were insane — cafe con leche (Cuban coffee and Oreos), Willy Cherino (bourbon and dark cherries), El Cochino Borracho (Jim Beam, candied bacon, and maple syrup), and passionfruit.

We ordered different ones just so we could try them all.

As I handed my cone to Evan to taste a drip, it felt effortless — like muscle memory.

Then Grace dropped the bomb.

"Tomorrow morning, we're going to Key West."

Evan blinked. "We are?"

She smiled. "David and I bought the tickets two days ago. Day trip. I thought I told you."

"You didn't," I said.

"Well... surprise!" she grinned. "Pack a change of clothes, a bathing suit, sunscreen. We'll meet in your lobby at 6:30."

Grace excused herself to call her son.

"Let's call Alex, too," I said.

He picked up on the first ring. "Hi Mom! Hi Dad!"

His tone was warm, if still a little cautious.

We caught up. He told us about the coach, about his stroke technique, about how he was being pushed toward real potential.

And then —

"Mom, Dad... at some point, I want to talk to Dr. Evan." He was trying to sound older. Grounded. "I won't yell. At least I'll try not to. But if there's a chance he might be around you... I want to talk to him."

David glanced at me before responding. "That's really mature, son. We can make that happen. End of the week okay?"

Alex nodded. "That's fine."

As he talked, I watched his face — his confidence — and it struck me.

Alex was stepping into his future.

And maybe it was time I started doing the same.

33

evan

The night air in Miami hit different after a day like today — sun, stories, and a little too much sugar. I wasn't sure what I expected when Mac said yes to this trip, but I didn't expect to be walking beside her like this. Comfortable. Easy. Like time hadn't passed.

By the time we reached the Ball & Chain, the street outside buzzed with people. The neon sign flickered over a line of tourists and locals queued up for Bachata Night. No cover, just music and sweat and the promise of dancing.

Inside, it was packed but not chaotic. A pulsing rhythm already filled the room — smooth, steady, laced with flirtation. Two instructors stood at the front: a man built like a shortstop and a woman who looked like she'd been dancing since birth. They were bantering with the DJ, running through final mic checks like this was a concert.

We found a space with a decent view and enough room to move. Grace and David were already trying out a few steps. Mac elbowed me gently and raised an eyebrow.

"You ready?" she said.

"Always," I replied, even though I hadn't danced bachata since med school, and even then, I was mediocre at best.

The instructors clapped to get everyone's attention, then jumped into basic steps — side to side, tap, repeat. Easy enough.

Until it wasn't.

Apparently, basic was just the warm-up. Within minutes, they layered in spins, hip flicks, syncopated turns. And Mac? She was eating it up — relaxed, playful, floating through every move like she'd done this a hundred times before.

I caught David's eye and mouthed, "She's done this before?"

He shrugged like it was obvious. "She goes out dancing. Alex told me."

I turned back to Mac, who met my glare with a wink. "You hustled me."

"Guilty," she said, grinning.

I laughed, shaking my head as I tried to keep up. "Man code violation, David."

"You'll live," he called over his shoulder.

Then came the partner work. The instructors paired us off, and Mac didn't hesitate. She laced her fingers through mine and pulled me toward the center.

"Let's show them how it's done," she said.

We settled into the rhythm, facing each other, steps mirroring. I focused on my feet — at least until I caught her eyes. Then all I could feel was the pull. Her laugh. Her hands in mine. Her body swaying in time with the beat — and with me.

She spun under my arm, then stepped in close. So close I could feel the heat of her skin and the rhythm of her breath. The air between us thickened. The music slowed — or maybe I just stopped paying attention to anything but her. She raised our hands again, turning under them, but I didn't let go. I brought her in — my hands slipping around her waist, pulling her against me.

Her hand was warm in mine, her breath brushing my collar. She didn't move away.

Neither did I.

Instead, I slid our hands behind her back and drew her even closer — flush against me. Her chest pressed into mine. Her lips parted just slightly.

And suddenly, the room fell away.

I wasn't thinking. I wasn't weighing consequences or what tomorrow might feel like. All I knew was that her mouth was right there — and I needed to know if she still tasted like home.

I kissed her.

It wasn't polite. It wasn't careful. It was fifteen years of ache, of unanswered questions, of what if we hadn't walked away. Her lips met mine with just as much urgency, just as much hunger. She kissed me like she needed this — like we both knew we weren't supposed to, but neither of us cared.

It didn't feel like a dance anymore. It felt like surrender.

When she pulled back, I could see it in her eyes — the confusion, the wanting, the fear. Her hands slid around my neck like she couldn't decide whether to let go or hold on tighter.

She kissed me again — deeper this time, bolder. And I let her. I let it all in. The years. The heat. The way her body fit against mine like we'd never stopped being us.

My hand slid down her back — muscle memory, pure instinct — until I was holding her the way I used to, the way I still remembered.

It scared me how much I still remembered.

Then a tap on my shoulder — and another — broke the spell.

Grace. David.

Mac pulled back like she'd just come up for air. "I— I need a second." Her voice was thin, breathless. She turned and disappeared into the crowd, heading for the restroom. Grace followed without a word.

I stood there, heart hammering.

This wasn't about the past anymore.

It never really was.

David stepped beside me, nodding toward the exit. "Outside. Now." I let him steer me out into the warm night, my head still spinning. He pointed to the curb, and I sat.

"You good?" he asked.

I exhaled. "I don't know what that was. It just — happened."

He raised an eyebrow. "You think?"

"I spent the day talking to her, reconnecting. I told myself I just wanted to see how she was doing. But tonight... I couldn't stop myself."

David shook his head. "Then don't pretend like that was just some casual kiss."

I didn't answer right away.

Because he was right.

The last time I kissed Mac like that, we were in our twenties — tipsy off homemade hot cocoa and the high of New Year's Eve. My mom had made pancakes at 3 a.m., and we were sitting in a hammock in the backyard, laughing like idiots as we tried to balance our plates. She offered me a bite — and I kissed her instead.

Soft. Careful. Like the world had gone quiet for a second.

That kiss had haunted me for years.
So had the silence that came after.

"I told her earlier that we should try to be friends," I said quietly.

David groaned. "And then you did that?"

"I panicked."

"Fix it tomorrow. Don't play with her — or yourself. Be honest about what you want."

I nodded, unsure what to say.

Back inside, Mac found me first. She didn't speak at first, just wrapped her arms around me in a quiet, grounding hug.

"It wasn't just you," she whispered. "I felt it too."

We didn't dance again. Didn't kiss again. But we stayed side by side the rest of the night.

And somehow, that felt more intimate than anything else.

34

david

After all the dancing and drama, we started the walk back to the car. Evan and Mac had a solid head start, already deep in whatever quiet moment they were sharing. Grace and I trailed behind, just close enough to observe — but far enough to keep the gossip private.

"Okay," I said, lowering my voice. "What the hell was that at Ball and Chain?"

Grace smirked. "That, my friend, was evidence that Operación Amor is officially a success."

"You do realize Evan talked her into a *just friends* situation, right?"

She rolled her eyes. "And clearly, that arrangement is hanging on by a thread. Did that look friendly to you?"

"Not even a little. And if they keep that up, we're going to get blacklisted from every respectable venue in Florida. I'd like to stay on *some* club guest lists."

Grace laughed. "Oh my God, calm down. You're acting like their loins set off a fire alarm."

"They almost did! That level of heat should be illegal in a public space."

"Who *says* stuff like that?" she groaned, covering her face. "My eyes. I need bleach. It's bedtime, and you're giving me Rated R visuals."

I grinned. "Blame my grandma. She used to say the most outrageous things — mostly aimed at me. I'm just passing it down, generational trauma style."

Grace snorted. "Anyway. They've kept it fairly chill so far, but tonight might've been a turning point."

"I'm not holding my breath. They've still got a long way to go."

"That's what Key West is for. Hopefully, they stop running from what's right in front of them and finally *deal* with it."

We rounded the corner and saw them already in the Tahoe. Second row. Sitting too close and pretending like they weren't.

"Look at them. Can't even wait for us to unlock the doors," I said.

We passed a convenience store still buzzing with clubgoers. The kind of place that stayed open until the last Uber left the block.

"I'm thirsty," I said. "We might as well grab water now."

Grace nodded. I jogged up to the car and stuck my head through the passenger window.

"Y'all want anything? We're grabbing drinks real quick."

Mac barely looked up. "Can't we just get water at the hotel?"

I shrugged. "This'll take two minutes. Chill."

She exhaled — loudly — but waved me off. Grace and I ducked into the store.

It was packed with folks fresh off the dance floor. We grabbed bottles of water and headed to the end of the line.

That's when my phone buzzed.

"Oh, hell," I muttered. "The woman I danced with tonight? She just texted. Wants to meet *right now.*"

Grace raised her brows. "You gave her your number?"

I gave her a look. "Just being polite. What — too risky?"

"Yes! That's not polite, that's a *booty call.* You don't even know if her husband's waiting at home with a shotgun!"

"I'm not that crazy," I muttered. "Estoy loco? No gracias."

Grace shook her head, laughing. "You better be careful. Meanwhile, that guy I danced with? Totally asked me out for coffee."

"You should go! Especially since your mysterious *boyfriend* hasn't even noticed you're out of town."

"Exactly. Radio silence. Can I ghost him? Is ghosting still a thing?"

I raised an eyebrow. "Define ghosting."

"Delete his number. Block his socials. Erase the call logs. Basically, act like he never existed."

"Damn — that's not ghosting, that's a full-blown disappearance."

She shrugged. "Might be for the best."

We finally reached the front of the line. I patted my pocket for my wallet...
and froze.

"Oh, shit."

"What?"

"I left the keys in the car. When I talked to Mac and Evan."

Grace's eyes widened. "You don't think they'd leave us, do you?"

"I mean... we *did* orchestrate their entire reunion."

We looked at each other — and bolted out of the store.

35

evan

I couldn't sleep once I got back to my hotel.

A late-night swim was tempting — but between the rum and the mojitos, I figured drunk drowning wasn't the legacy I wanted to leave behind. The pool didn't have a lifeguard anyway, and I wasn't about to become some sad headline.

What I needed to do was figure out the Mac situation.

I'm the one who opened the door to "let's just be friends." So now, kissing her? It probably felt like I was trying to backdoor my way into something casual — not something real. And maybe that was part of it. But David was right. If I wanted something different, I needed to be honest — with her and with myself.

Key West would give me that window.

If I didn't fumble it.

Grace and I met in the lobby at 5:40 AM.

I looked like a poor excuse for the man I was trying to be — and Grace, of course, let me know.

She kissed my cheek, eyeing me head to toe in her crisp white jumpsuit and flats. "Damn. You look worse than hell — and comparing you to shit is unfair to shit. Did you even shower?"

"Of course I showered. I just need coffee. I spent the night thinking about Mac."

Grace sighed. "Maybe instead of all that thinking, you should've prepped for doing. Because if she sees you looking like this? She might hit you with a hard pass."

She shoved me toward the breakfast nook like a mom on a mission.

I grabbed a muffin. She grabbed three.

"Did you talk to David?" I asked.

"Oh, I did. I cannot believe you fumbled your way into a friends-only corner. I swear, you used to be smooth."

While she was roasting me, she was also scanning the coffee bar. She handed me a travel mug. "Drink this before you embarrass both of us."

I took a sip and perked up instantly. "Why do you even have a mug for me?"

"Well, it was Gabe's old water mug. But since the Swim Academy gave him a new one, I reclaimed this one. And honestly? You need it more than he does today."

I nodded. "Thanks. Let's grab food and go meet David and Mac."

She pointed a banana at me like it was a warning. "Big day, Evan. Don't blow it."

Twenty minutes later, we pulled up to their hotel about 6 AM. David was already in the lobby. Mac was at the front desk.

I saw her before she saw me — and just like that, the nerves came flooding back. She looked beautiful. Radiant, even. This early in the morning. Unfair. The hotel had a coffee bar in the lobby. As soon as I offered to grab drinks, Mac walked over with me.

"You look amazing this morning," I said, refilling my mug. "No one would guess you were out late partying."

She smiled, tired. "Thanks. But looks can be deceiving. I think we're officially too old for late-night hangs. No latte for you?"

"I need something stronger today. I've got a lot on my mind."

"Clearly." She took a sip from the cup I handed her — immediately frowned — then reached for the milk. "Nope. I still need milk. Some things never change."

Grace joined us, eyeing the coffee tray. "Not bad. Not great. Passable." She poured David a cup even though he was still on the phone across the room. He waved her off, and she poured one anyway.

"So where's this bus?" Mac asked.

"Meet point's around the corner," Grace replied. "Check-in at 6:30, departure at 7:00. Bus is actually decent — for a bus. But just in case, I brought muffins, bananas, and meds. No stomach drama in Key West today."

Mac peeked into Grace's bag and then darted off toward the buffet. "Be right back!"

I laughed. Grace gave me a knowing look. "I can't wait until y'all figure it out. All these longing stares? Makes me want to delete every man I've ever met. Matter of fact — I did. Last night. Deleted him. Gone."

I raised an eyebrow. She shrugged.

"I want what you and Mac had — or maybe still have. And I'm not wasting time on halfway love anymore."

I didn't feel like a role model. But I wasn't about to dim her hope either.

Mac returned, grinning. "Check this out."

She opened her bag like a kid showing off Halloween candy.

I laughed. "Is there enough for me?"

"If you play your cards right."

We took an Uber to the meet point and joined the boarding line. The bus was plush — spacious and half full. Grace curled up with a paperback. David settled in to nap. Mac and I claimed seats near the back.

She leaned her head back, exhaling hard. "I could nap. We've been on the move nonstop. This is what a vacation's supposed to feel like?"

"This ride won't be relaxing. We need to talk."

Mac cracked one eye open. "Didn't we already talk?"

"We said we'd try to be friends — at least."

She repeated it softly. "At least."

I pushed on. "That means actually knowing each other. You're a whole person I've missed for fifteen years. That's a lot of time. And I want to know you — now. What your life looks like. What you want."

She didn't say anything at first. Then, without opening her eyes: "I do know we both managed to be unhappily married to really nice people. Maybe we're just not marriage material."

"I don't believe that. If we had stayed together... I think we'd still be married. Maybe even with kids."

She finally looked at me. "Can you imagine if all of them had your hair?"

I chuckled. "Disaster — especially for a daughter. Took me forty years to figure out mine."

She reached out, gently ran her hand through it. "Still feels the same. You used to use that coconut shampoo, right?"

I smiled. "Because you liked the smell."

Her eyes lit up. "Really? You bought coconut products just for me?"

I nodded, suddenly shy.

"If we were still together," she said, leaning back, "that would've earned you a sexy thank you. But since we're just friends — I'll say thank you instead."

"Ouch," I said, teasing.

She smirked. "Cruel because it's mean — or cruel because it turned you on?"

"Don't answer that," she added before I could open my mouth.

And then — just to mess with me — she crossed her legs and her skirt shifted.

I tried to focus. "You've changed your hair too. I like it."

"Braids are easier with swimming. Healthier. No more chemical burns."

"They suit you."

"Thanks. Oop — looks like a breakfast stop. You want anything?"

I shook my head. She didn't leave either.

"I'm glad you stayed," she said quietly, tucking her legs beneath her.

"I like being around you." I looked at her fully. "There's still so much we don't know."

She turned toward me. "Tell me about your practice."

"It's everything I hoped. Chief resident. Research. I stayed after residency. I operate two days a week. Clinics two days. Half-day admin. I even teach gross anatomy once a semester."

She smiled. "I always wanted to see you operate. Never got the chance."

"Why?"

"You loved it. Your third-year neurosurg rotation? You were lit up. It was sexy."

Before I could respond, David walked by. "Don't forget to pick your excursions. We've got about six hours in Key West."

Grace stirred as he went by, shot him a dirty look, then passed back out.

I looked at Mac again. "You seem more comfortable in your skin now."

She nodded. "After us, I had to pull myself together. It took a while. But I focused on residency. On surviving."

She paused. Then: "I missed you. For a long time. That's probably why I... ended up with David."

I didn't say anything.

I wasn't sure I wanted to know what came next.

36

mackenzie

Talking to Evan about David wasn't exactly the sexiest thing in the world, but the truth was — we wouldn't be here without him. That whole relationship forced me to grow up. It taught me how to stop avoiding the hard parts and actually deal with my emotions instead of running from them.

"I went to Vegas toward the end of my second year. Couple residents were with me. Everyone else hooked up with someone, and I had been drinking. That's when I met David. He was drunk too. We got married that night."

Evan shook his head, smirking. "Still wild to me."

"I was looking for something to fill the space. It was supposed to be fun. Just a weekend thing. Then I got pregnant, and everything shifted. He wanted to raise the baby, and I wanted a stable life. But we were never in love."

He nodded slowly. "Feels familiar. Grace and I worked a case together. I was lonely and grieving, and she looked like the right kind of next step. But she wasn't you. So we ended it."

He reached for my hand, brushing his thumb over the inside of my wrist.

"Having Alex made me step up. There was no time to waste worrying about how I looked or who liked me. I had a baby to protect, to raise, to prepare for the world. And in doing that, I started to understand my mother in ways I never could before."

"It's amazing how fast your world shrinks down to one person," he said. "And how fast it expands again once they start to pull away."

"Yeah. That's where I am. I don't have a plan for myself after Alex leaves. I've been thinking about it more and more on this trip."

"You still have your practice. Friends. A whole life."

"But is that enough?" I asked. "Do I want more kids? I don't know. And if I do, I'm running out of time to figure that out."

He nodded. "I haven't thought much about dating again either. Most of my focus has been on Gabe — raising him right, keeping him steady. But this week... it's changed a few things for me."

I tilted my head. "Changed how?"

He didn't look away. "I don't think I want to be just friends."

That hit me square in the chest. My eyes stung, and I wasn't sure what to say.

We sat in silence for a moment and I rested my head on his shoulder. He placed a hand on my thigh, gentle and grounding. And that was the end of my nap attempt.

Ten minutes in, he tapped me.

"You sleeping?"

"Not anymore."

"I just don't want to waste time. It's been fifteen years, Mac."

He was watching me again, the way he used to—like I was something he hadn't tasted in too long.

"So," I said slowly, "you remember that first night? After the rescue?"

He grinned. "You mean when you brought dinner in that clingy green dress and tried to pretend it was just a thank-you?"

"It *was* a thank-you."

"Mmhm." He smirked, letting his hand slide slowly up my thigh — past the hem of my sundress and right toward the crease he used to know better than I knew it myself. "You wore that dress on purpose. You knew exactly what you were doing."

I swallowed hard. "And what am I doing now?"

He leaned in, whispering so close to my ear it made my whole body shiver.

"Making me remember how good your pussy used to feel wrapped around me."

The moan that escaped me was half-laugh, half-desperate plea. I was *done* pretending. All this slow burn, this teasing back and forth — it was over. My thighs were already pressed together, aching from anticipation. My panties felt ruined.

I stood up without a word, walked to the back of the bus, and slipped into the tiny bathroom.

My reflection looked just as wrecked as I felt — flushed cheeks, bitten lips, eyes glassy with want.

Then the door opened — and Evan stepped inside.

There was no hesitation. No nervous energy. He locked the door and turned to me like a man starving.

I grabbed the collar of his shirt and dragged him down into a kiss — the kind that felt more like inhaling than kissing. His mouth crashed into mine and I could taste the coffee on his tongue — hot and a little sweet — and I knew right then I was going to let him fuck me until I cried.

His hands were all over me — cupping my ass, dragging my dress up to my waist. I gasped when he slid his thigh between mine, pressing against me right where I needed him most.

"Still so goddamn responsive," he growled against my mouth.

"You haven't even done anything yet."

"Oh baby," he said, slipping his hand into my thong and groaning when his fingers found just how wet I was, "you sure about that?"

He slipped two fingers inside and my knees buckled.

"Fuck—Evan—"

"You feel exactly the same. Maybe tighter." He curved his fingers, finding that spot that made my eyes roll back. "You miss this?"

"Y-yes—oh my God—"

He pumped in and out slowly, deliberately, while his thumb circled my clit. I braced myself against the wall, trying not to whimper like a damn schoolgirl.

"Not yet," he whispered. "You're not coming until I'm inside you."

He pulled his fingers out and brought them to his mouth — sucking them clean while looking me dead in the eyes.

I moaned, knees shaking. "You are *so* full of yourself."

"And you're full of me in about ten seconds."

I reached for his belt, desperate now. "Pants. Off. Now."

He kissed me again as I undid his fly, tugging his shorts down. His dick sprang free — thick, hard, veiny, and familiar enough to make my stomach drop.

"Oh my *God*, Evan."

"You remember?" he asked, gripping the base and stroking once, slow and mean.

"Of course I remember. I used to ride that thing like my fucking life depended on it."

"Well." He turned me around and bent me over the tiny sink. "Let's get reacquainted."

I heard the tear of a wrapper, and then — warmth. One hand at my waist, the other spreading me open like I was something to be *savored*.

"I've thought about this so many times," he murmured, lining up behind me. "Dreamed about being back inside you."

He pushed in — slow at first — just the head.

I gasped so loud I slapped a hand over my mouth.

He grunted. "Still. So. Fucking. Tight."

He pushed deeper. Inch by inch. Until I felt him fill me completely — stretching me out like he owned the space.

"Oh, *fuck*," I moaned into my hand. "I forgot—how *deep* you get—Jesus—"

"I didn't." He gripped my hips and pulled back, then slammed forward again. My thighs hit the sink. My whole body rocked.

"I can feel every part of you," I panted. "God, Evan—it's *so good*—"

He picked up the pace, his strokes long and purposeful — not just fucking me, but *reminding* me what it was like to be ruined by him.

"You like that?" he growled. "You want me to keep fucking you like this?"

"Don't stop—don't *you dare* stop—"

"You're so fucking wet—I can hear it." He punctuated each word with a thrust. "You missed this. You missed me."

I was already close — again — just from the sound of him, the *feel* of him.

"Come on, Mac," he said, voice low and rough. "Come on my dick. Let me feel you fall apart for me."

I did.

It hit fast and violent — clenching, pulsing, my back arching as I fought not to scream. He held me through it, still fucking me, chasing his own orgasm now.

"Gonna fill you up," he panted. "Even with the condom—I wanna feel you milk me dry—fuck—you're still so perfect—"

"Do it," I begged. "*Do it*, Evan—"

He growled, drove in one final time, and came — hard — slamming his hips into mine as he emptied himself inside the condom.

We stayed like that for a long moment — his forehead on my back, both of us breathless.

Then he slowly pulled out, rolling the condom off and tossing it. I turned to face him, and he kissed me again — softer this time.

"Still got it," he whispered.

"You never *lost* it."

He grinned and crouched down, gently wiping between my thighs with a paper towel — but not before kissing the inside of my knee like he was worshiping it.

I sagged back against the sink. "You're gonna kill me."

"Nah," he said, helping me pull my panties up. "I'm just getting started."

37

mackenzie

I didn't get a lot of looks or giggles as I made my way back to our seat, but it *felt* like every person on the bus was looking at me. It was probably my imagination. Still — I might as well have had a "just got fucked" sign stamped on my forehead.

I slid into my seat by the window and sank as low as I could.

Evan grinned. "You're blushing like after our first kiss at my grandmother's party. There was nothing to be ashamed of then either."

I groaned, covering my face.

Before I could mentally will myself to disappear, my phone beeped. It was Grace.

Grace

> How was it?

Me

> How was what?

Grace

> I saw your walk of shame from the bathroom.

> So, are you two back together? Or was that just an itch?

Me

> I don't know what you're talking about.

Grace

Lol sure.

With each message, my face got hotter.

"Who are you texting? Grace?" Evan asked, trying to peek over my shoulder.

I cut my eyes at him. "She texted me *first*. She somehow *knows* what happened in the bathroom. So, everyone probably heard us. I don't know why I'm so embarrassed — I thought I was past caring what people think."

Evan kissed my cheek. "Remember, you're a grown, vibrant woman. Nobody can say anything to you. You're a badass. I remember how scared you were that my folks would hate you."

I tried not to smile — *tried*. Evan had invited me home with him for Christmas that first year. At the time, I figured it was just because I didn't have family nearby. But there was more to it than that — he'd had a whole plan.

His grandmother was turning 100 on New Year's Eve, and his entire family had gathered for the celebration. The parties, the chaos, the noise — it was a whirlwind I hadn't been used to. My family was smaller. Quieter.

And then came midnight.

He pulled me into a hallway right before the countdown ended. Folded me into his arms like it was the most natural thing in the world.

"Happy New Year," he said softly. "May you get everything you want this year and more."

I smiled. "Same to you."

Then, a little tipsy, I'd dared to ask, "What did you wish for?"

He looked right at me. "You."

My breath caught.

"I've wanted to kiss you for months," he confessed. "Your mouth, Mac... the things I've imagined those lips doing. I'm drunk — that's the only reason I'm saying this out loud. If you want me to back off, I will—"

But I didn't let him finish. I stood on my toes and kissed him first.

The kiss was soft at first. Careful. He tasted like champagne and vanilla, and when he deepened it, when his tongue slid against mine, I swore I could feel the way my life was about to change.

His hand curled into my hair. My hips pressed into his. I could feel him, hard and ready, even through his slacks.

And then —

"Excuse me..."

Liza and her fiancé, Stephon, were standing there, both smirking.

"It's about time," Liza said, cocking her head. "You might want to take that upstairs."

I fled to the powder room, cheeks burning. One look in the mirror told me everything — flushed face, swollen lips, hair a mess. Liza hadn't been wrong.

That night had been the start of *everything.* But even then, the cynical part of me — the one that had been alone most holidays before Evan — wondered if this was temporary. If I was just a warm body to kiss at midnight.

It took time for me to believe I wasn't a placeholder. That I *was* what he wanted.

And now, all these years later, that same voice was back. Whispering. Wondering.

Was this nostalgia? A one-week rerun of Evan 'n Mac before we returned to regular programming?

I didn't want to be reckless with my heart. But I also didn't want to cut this short.

I didn't know where we'd end up — only that right now, I didn't want it to be over.

"Hey — are you with me?" Evan tapped my shoulder. "Where'd you go?"

I blinked. "Sorry. Just took a little trip down memory lane."

He laughed. "You still look like you're worried someone's judging you. Mac... people who give you weird looks? They're jealous. Everyone wants someone who makes them *scream.* Just relax. Besides David and Grace, who else on this bus do we even know?"

I covered my face again. "I hate you."

He kissed the side of my head. "No, you don't."

I tried to pivot. "So — what do we want to do in Key West? Snorkeling? Hemingway House? Glass bottom boat tour?" I flipped through the brochure. "We only have six hours."

"Hemingway, for sure. I wouldn't mind the boat, either. David mentioned wanting to do that one."

I pulled out my phone and texted him.

> Hey, thinking of doing the glass bottom boat tour. You in?

David

> Absolutely.

> Cool. They have a 1 PM slot wanna just book together?

David

> I'll book for both of us. My treat. Consider it a thank-you for not letting Grace blow the itinerary budget at Ball & Chain.

> Ha! Fair. Thank you. You're the best co-parent.

David

> And don't you forget it.

I dropped my phone back in my bag and sighed. "I need a nap."

"Come here," Evan said, shifting so I could lean against him.

I curled into the space under his arm — the space I'd once known better than my own bed — and let myself rest there.

Maybe this didn't need a label. Not yet. Maybe it was enough, for now, just to be close again.

And maybe, just maybe, I'd finally let myself enjoy it.

38

evan

Mac slept for the last hour of the ride. I was jealous — desperate, even — for that kind of peace, but my mind wouldn't let me rest.

So instead, I watched her.

Every few minutes, I glanced out the window as we made our way along the Seven-Mile Bridge — blue water stretching endlessly in either direction, like we were driving straight into the horizon. But mostly, my eyes stayed on her. Mac, curled against my shoulder, breathing evenly, her lashes casting soft shadows. She looked peaceful — the same woman who once couldn't set foot on a beach without breaking into a full-blown anxiety attack.

When we finally reached Key West, Mac stirred, blinking groggily and sitting up with a little jolt. She was still waking up as the bus came to a stop. I grabbed her hand when she nearly stumbled on the last step, steadying her. I didn't let go.

David and Grace had already gotten off — they were up a few rows ahead. They spotted us the second we stepped down.

Grace waved. "Whew, girl! You look like you haven't slept in days. What's going on?"

Mac, blushing but composed, said, "Rough bus trip. I just need to freshen up. Where are we supposed to go for the boat tour? What time does it start?"

Smooth redirect. Classic Mac.

Grace took the hint and backed off. David, on the other hand...

He slapped my palm and grinned. "Dude! I didn't know you had it in you. Is there a name for fucking on a bus? Sexo en un autobús? El club de las tierras planas?"

Each one made me laugh — and blush harder.

Grace opened her translation app. "Are these real phrases? Can I use them in public and not get arrested? I'm adding them to my list of obscene things to say in Spanish."

That made Mac laugh. Which made me smile.

Key West was hot — in the best way. That first wave of salt air and blinding sunshine hit as soon as we stepped off the bus. I dug in my bag for sunglasses, took in the palm trees, the pastel storefronts, the steel drum rhythm that floated faintly on the breeze. This place had charm — loud, sweaty, wild charm — but charm all the same.

We regrouped and made our way over to the tour guide kiosk. The guy working it — tatted, young, probably just here for the summer — pointed us toward the dock at Mallory Square. It was a short walk, and we weren't alone. A whole pack of tourists were heading the same way.

Still holding Mac's hand, I glanced over at her. She lifted our joined hands and smiled.

"So, the bus bathroom was the beginning of a new era?"

I raised an eyebrow. "Maybe. Or maybe it's the return of an old one."

She looked at me, searching. "What do you mean?"

"I just mean... we're gonna have to talk about what this is. What we want it to be. But either way — I plan to make love to you in much better places than a bus." I kissed her hand.

She smiled again, but it didn't quite reach her eyes. There was uncertainty there — in her, and if I was being honest, in me too. But that didn't change how I felt about being here, in this moment. I was going to make the most of every single second.

Grace turned around. "Anyone hungry? I've still got a snack or two in my bag. We can stop and grab something to eat now — or after the boat ride. I wanna hit Margaritaville later. Or one of those iconic Key West bars that have dollar bills stapled to the ceiling."

We ducked into a convenience store for snacks and drinks — nothing fancy. Just something to get us through the boat ride. I paid. Mac slipped a granola bar into her bag.

Once we reached the dock, we still had about thirty minutes to kill before the tour started. The four of us grabbed a spot on a bench nearby, watching the foot traffic and sunbathers and all the other people-watching gold Key West had to offer.

A couple from our bus — Milo and Sara — sat down next to us and struck up a conversation. They were newlyweds from outside Miami, honeymooning on a budget.

"You've been here before?" Milo asked, looking between all of us.

David nodded. "I have. A few times. The rest of them — not so much."

"I've technically been here," Mac said, "but I was a new mom. I don't remember anything except formula and spit-up and being tired."

She shot David a look. "And a thirty-year-old man to take care of."

David gasped. "I resent that implication. I was twenty-nine, thank you — and I was taking care of you."

Mac rolled her eyes. "Sure you were."

Sara leaned in. "Do y'all have any recommendations? Like, real ones? Not the tourist ones."

We all exchanged a look — the kind that said, Where do we even start?

"We're about to blow your mind," Grace said with a grin.

We explained. The co-parenting. The exes. The trip. The fact that none of us were married — at least, not anymore — but still managed to function like a dysfunctional Brady Bunch. Milo and Sara sat there, mouths open.

"I really thought the pairings were different," Sara said, glancing between us. "Y'all are like... too functional. I love it. You should have a reality show!"

Milo snorted. "No one would watch. Not enough drama. Do you throw dishes? Slam doors?"

"No dish throwing," Grace said, "but I do slam a mean door."

"I pick up women. Unmarried ones," David added.

They laughed. So did we.

"You have no idea," David said, sitting back with a smile.

39

mackenzie

The boat captain paused at the ticket booth before stepping onto the glass-bottom boat docked at the pier.

"We'll be leaving soon," Grace said, holding up a packet of Dramamine. "If anyone gets seasick, speak now or forever hold your vomit. I'm not trying to hear anyone retching and set mine off."

Nobody took her up on it. Hopefully, we wouldn't regret that.

Evan glanced over at me. "Crazy how you used to only get in the water by accident."

I gave him a small smile — but the memory hit harder than expected. It wasn't just a throwback. It was *the* moment. The one that rewrote everything.

"I was just thinking about that day," I said.

He nodded, his expression soft. "Are you okay?"

"Yeah — just felt like I was back there for a second. I could smell the chlorine. I swear I could almost *touch* them."

Evan leaned in slightly. "Do you want water or something?"

I shook my head. "No. Just — give me a minute."

I closed my eyes and let the sensation pass, even though a small part of me hoped for more. Another glimpse. Another second.

"I never told you what I saw," I said after a pause. "Back then. When I almost died — or *died*, I don't know what to call it." I made air quotes around the word.

"You didn't," he said gently. "You've thanked me in a lot of ways, but you never mentioned seeing anything. I'd like to hear about it."

"I saw my parents," I said. "Like — actually *saw* them. My mom looked peaceful for the first time in years. My dad looked just like I remembered. They were together. Whole. And I was walking toward them. I *wanted* to go."

I hesitated, glancing at him.

"But then I heard your voice. You were calling me back. So I came."

Evan blinked — stunned. "You *heard* me?"

I nodded.

He leaned back on the bench, eyes wide. "I thought I imagined everything I said to you. That none of it mattered. But I just — I knew you couldn't die. We had just met, and I didn't know what you meant to me yet, but I *felt* it. I needed you."

That cracked something open in my chest.

I leaned in and kissed him — soft, sure.

That was it. That's why so much of my life had felt off since we broke up. I needed him — even his annoying optimism. I'd been so scared of falling apart that I didn't trust us to survive it. And once I got better, I never circled back to try again. I let the door close without even knocking.

Years — gone. And I hated how much of that was on me.

A tear slipped out before I could stop it. Evan caught it with his thumb.

"Hey. Don't cry," he said gently. "We've still got time. As long as we're breathing, we've got time to fix this."

It was the first time he'd said it out loud — *fix us*. And that alone made it easier to believe.

Once we boarded, Grace started tossing out snacks like she was coaching a kids' soccer team. The crew side-eyed us while trying to sell overpriced chips, but the adult beverages moved quick — and we all got one.

As the boat pulled away from the dock, I found myself glued to the water. Dolphins, manatees, sea turtles, tuna, even a few types of sharks drifted by. The marine guide listed them off like a catalog, his voice calm and practiced.

A woman near us mentioned a close call with a nurse shark while kayaking. I shuddered. They weren't aggressive, but still — a plastic kayak was not enough between me and *any* kind of shark.

Evan lit up. "We should've gone snorkeling!"

I raised a brow.

"I'll go with Gabe. Or Alex and David. They'd be down."

"Better," I said, touching his face. "But you better not let my child get eaten. My ex? He's on his own."

Evan looked at David, who shrugged. "She's the boss."

I smiled, sinking into the moment. There was something peaceful about watching sea life glide by — like nothing else existed. I *knew* that wasn't their reality. I knew their lives were full of predators and survival instincts. But from this side of the glass, it was pure serenity.

I had to be practically dragged off the boat.

Not that Milo and Sara noticed. They were making out the whole ride. Evan and I didn't go that far — but we did hold hands the entire time. He leaned in every so often, whispering random facts about the fish in my ear like some sexy marine biologist. It was hot.

But we weren't hooking up in any more public bathrooms. I still had a bruise from the bus sink. That spot had edges.

Besides — I wasn't trying to stay in this "friends" limbo much longer.

"Where are we eating? I'm starving," David said as we disembarked.

"I vote Duval Street," I replied. "Everything's there."

"Somewhere with good drinks," Grace added. "I need another." She shot David a wink.

Hmm.

What's she up to now?

Evan and I had clocked their nosiness about our reunion — but this felt more... pointed.

They were planning something.

And that meant we needed to stay ready.

40

mackenzie/evan

"What time do we need to get back to the bus?" I asked, leaning back in my chair. "I think I ate everything on my plate — and yours — and probably swiped a few bites from strangers."

"You've made a mockery of moderation today," David said, raising an eyebrow. "I don't think I've ever seen you eat like that. Not even when you were pregnant. You were a machine."

"It was all *so* good. I just let myself enjoy it."

Evan leaned in and whispered, "You're going to need that energy later."

I laughed. "Same for you."

Grace rolled her eyes. "Ugh. You two. I bet you were unbearable when you were actually together. The sex just rolls off you in waves. Disgusting."

David raised his beer and clinked her glass. "They're sickening, right? And as for the *actual* relationship — guess we'll wait and see."

Evan cleared his throat. "We're friends. It's nice to be back in that space. I missed her."

I didn't flinch on the outside — but inside, I shriveled. That was too firm. Too final. Like he'd already decided what this was *and wasn't*. Couldn't he have left the door cracked?

And honestly, part of me just wanted the week to be over. If this didn't work out — if I had to go home and carry this heartbreak *again* — it would take me forever to climb out. But being with him now, even temporarily, still felt worth it.

"Oh crap! We need to get back!" Evan checked his watch. "Our six hours are almost up."

David stood and stretched. "Yep. Especially since some of us need to work off everything we just inhaled."

That was for me. I stood and attempted a graceful sashay — but it ended up more of a flounce. Their laughter followed me all the way to the street.

We made our way to the pick-up spot. The sun had worn us down, and the food didn't help. A line had started to form, and Evan and I joined the back. Grace and David were hanging back, whispering to each other.

I nudged Evan. "What are they up to?"

He shrugged and turned to David. "Can I get our tickets? I want to grab a coffee before we leave."

David and Grace exchanged glances — *weird* glances.

"What?" I said slowly. "What's going on?"

David scratched the back of his neck — and wouldn't meet my eyes. That was *never* a good sign.

"What is it, David?"

"We have some news for you..." he said, drawing it out like I wasn't seconds away from popping off.

I crossed my arms and sighed loud enough to make a point. Evan slipped an arm around my shoulders, trying to steady whatever storm he sensed brewing.

Grace jumped in. "You don't have a ticket back to Miami tonight. You have one for tomorrow afternoon." She smiled like this was a birthday surprise. "Surprise!"

Evan chuckled. "Funny." But when he saw their expressions, his smile dropped. "Wait — you're *serious*?"

Grace and David didn't say a word.

"What the fuck?" Evan stepped forward. "You didn't buy us return tickets? Why the fuck not?"

My jaw dropped. Of course this was part of some elaborate setup.

David jumped in before I could start cussing in two languages. "Hear us out, querida — la madre de mi hijo." He gave me his best innocent face. "You two have a couple days left to figure this out. And the bus bathroom this morning doesn't count. You need space. No distractions. I booked you a room at a nice resort for the night. Consider it an apology gift."

He shrugged. "Yo lo siento?"

"Have a good time," Grace added. "Maybe you'll have some answers tomorrow."

She stepped toward Evan and kissed his cheek — whispering something I couldn't hear — then hugged me before I could decide whether to cuss her out or hug her back.

David must've decided her survival meant it was safe to approach. He stepped up, took both of my hands, and raised them to his face.

"I only want what's best for you. For *Alex* too. This — this could be it. Please try."

He kissed my hands and backed away.

Touching. Still shady.

Clearly sensing the end of their grace period, Grace and David hustled into the line — quickly. Probably for their own safety. I didn't want to explain to Alex why I had to finish off his father in a Key West alley.

As I watched them board, I spotted a few familiar faces from this morning. And while I was still salty about being duped, part of me didn't mind the extra time with Evan.

The deception? Annoying.

The outcome? I'd take it.

Evan

When Grace kissed my cheek, she whispered, "Please use this time wisely. Enjoy it. Try to find a way forward."

She knew me too well.

As it sank in that Mac and I were alone — *truly* alone — I felt a flicker of hope. Maybe this was it. My shot to stop playing this *friends* game and finally say what I actually felt.

But I still didn't know how to bring it up without shattering what we were just starting to rebuild.

A ping came through on my phone — a text from David with our return tickets for tomorrow and a reservation at the Havana Cabana. It looked stunning. Bright, comfortable, and way too nice to have been booked on short notice unless this had been planned *well* in advance.

Mac peeked over my shoulder. "That hotel looks amazing," she said, her voice soft but amused. "We'll stay tonight. But I don't want to spend the whole trip in bed — tempting as that is. I want to see Duval Street. I've heard it's magic at night."

She winked. "I'll make it worth your while."

It already was.

41

mackenzie/evan

With Duval Street as our home base for the night, there was plenty of mischief to get into. I giggled to myself, thinking maybe we'd get drunk and find a justice of the peace. That might be the only way I ever get to my own wedding.

"What's so funny?" Evan asked, wrapping his arms around me.

"Nothing," I said, kissing him lightly. "Okay — we've got to make some plans. I want to take a sunset cruise. That cool with you?"

Evan looked straight into my eyes. "I'd love that. Though I might have a hard time focusing on the sunset with the most beautiful, sexy woman standing next to me."

I couldn't help the grin that spread across my face. "Where do we go to reserve seats? Hopefully it's not sold out."

"Ask the bus guy," Evan said. "Pretty sure he handles the extracurriculars."

Then he leaned in and murmured, "Well... not *all* of them."

His breath on my neck made my knees soft and my underwear damp. I *wanted* to see the sights — really — but Evan was making that hard. I wasn't trying to be the girl who only wanted to get laid... but damn if it wasn't tempting.

I turned toward him and said, "I'm *still* embarrassed that everybody heard us. You know I don't do public displays like that. But if you keep breathing on me like that, I will mount you right here. I don't care if I get arrested. It'll be worth the mugshot."

He blushed and kissed my cheek. "Public indecency isn't a felony. But if you want to test that theory..."

I shot him a look.

"Fine, fine," he said, holding up his hands. "Gun holstered — for now. But you better be ready to back that talk up later."

I shivered. Oh, I had plans.

We found the event scheduler near the dock, and thank God — there were two spots left for the last sunset cruise of the evening. Walking back toward Duval, I felt giddy. A night in Key West, on somebody else's dime, with the man I never really stopped loving. It felt like something out of a story. No judgement. No regrets.

Evan squeezed my hand, and I knew he was feeling it too.

The night was wide open.

Getting on the boat, Evan asked the captain about the route.

"This one's under two hours," the captain said. "You'll see a few landmarks, hear a little history, then be back in time for dinner or nightlife. You picked a perfect night — skies are clear, sunset's gonna be beautiful."

He wasn't lying. The sky looked painted in streaks of pink, orange, and gold. A single cloud hovered over the sun like a pillow waiting to catch it as it dipped into the ocean. I couldn't speak. It was that beautiful.

Evan led me to two open seats, and I immediately turned to watch the sun drop.

"I don't care what else they show us — that sunset is everything. I need a picture. I want to remember this... how it *feels*."

"You won't forget," Evan started. "This could be—"

But just then, the captain called for everyone to take a seat as we pulled out of the dock. The first mate — a young woman in her thirties — introduced herself and gave a brief rundown of safety protocols. I appreciated that. I'd worked hard to get past my fear of water, but I still needed a plan just in case.

During the first half of the cruise, we passed famous sites, each one pointed out by the first mate. Evan and I stayed close, occasionally pulling out our phones to look up more info. At one point, we passed a small island dotted with beautiful homes.

"That's Sunset Key," the first mate said.

With the sun behind it, it looked unreal. My breath caught.

We'd talked about getting married on an island. Catalina. At sunset. Surrounded by our family and friends. That dream never made it past the planning stages. But standing here, looking at *this* view — it hit me. That could've been us.

Evan must've felt it too. He wrapped his arms around my waist and kissed the side of my head.

"It's not over," he said quietly. "We can still have everything we dreamed of. All of it's still out there."

"We could find a justice of the peace tonight," I whispered before I could stop myself.

He didn't laugh. Didn't tease.

"When we're ready," he said, "I'll marry you anywhere you want."

I leaned into him. And for once, the memory didn't hurt. It just... settled. It felt safe — like I used to feel with him. Like I *could* again.

The second half of the cruise shifted from sentimental to celebration. The stewards opened the bar — champagne, beer, cocktails — and passed around trays of food. Music blasted from the speakers, and people started dancing. The vibe was pure Jimmy Buffett and Key West chaos.

We joined in — champagne in hand, slightly tipsy.

"Let's look up Jimmy Buffett," Evan said, spinning me around. "Some of these songs sound familiar."

I spilled a little champagne on myself. "Still a messy drinker, huh?" he teased.

"Adds to my charm."

I hummed along with the next song. "I *do* know this one. What'd Google say?"

"Not from here, but he spent a lot of time in Key West. Made it his home base. Started his restaurant chain here. I think there's a resort, too."

He pulled me in close. Even with all the noise, it felt like we were the only two people on the boat.

I tilted my head up. The kiss was soft. Deep. Familiar. When his lips touched mine, I knew he was my destiny.

But was I his?

And was I brave enough to find out?

Later, as we stood by the railing watching the sky shift from bright to dusky blues, I felt a peace I hadn't felt in years. Evan took me as I was — even back then, when I didn't have my shit together. I wasn't that girl anymore, fragile and guilt-ridden. But I still had baggage. And regrets.

I remembered how I pulled away after his dad died. How I didn't show up. Who *does* that to someone they love?

Could he trust me again?

"A penny for your thoughts?"

I couldn't say all of that. Not here. Not now. So I gave him a smile and leaned in.

"They're impure," I purred. "I think I've seen enough of Duval Street. Let's see the inside of that hotel David so generously paid for."

We grabbed a Lyft to the resort. Pulling up, it looked like something straight out of *The Godfather Part II* — palm trees, vintage cars, pastel buildings with an old-school Cuban vibe.

"Think anyone gets to ride in those cars?" Evan asked, admiring one of the old Chevys.

"Something to ask at the front desk."

A sign near the entrance confirmed it was a 21+ resort and boasted the largest pool in Key West. Too bad we only had one night to enjoy it.

"We've *got* to come back," I said.

Evan just squeezed my hand.

"We have a reservation under Evan Robertson," he told the clerk.

The night clerk pulled up our info and smiled. "You're in a premium room — ocean-facing, king bed, private balcony."

He was about to hand us our keys... then paused.

"Hold on — there's a note here. We need about 10 minutes before your room is ready."

He flagged a maid, whispered something to her, and she rushed off.

"I'm so sorry for the delay," the clerk said. "Can I offer you water — or a mojito coupon for the pool bar?"

We took the coupons and sat in the lobby. Evan wandered over to the gift shop.

"Some of these future stay packages are wild. One comes with condoms and body butter."

I joined him. "Noted."

Ten minutes later, the maid returned and gave a small nod. The clerk stood and motioned for us to follow.

Evan looked at me — really looked — and that glance said everything. Past. Present. Possibility.

He gave my hand a squeeze and led me to the elevator. His arm stayed draped over my shoulders, fingers tracing lazy circles on my skin.

The clerk opened the door to our suite.

Inside... was a dream.

A trail of rose petals led to the bed. The word *love* was spelled out in petals across the duvet. Two bottles of champagne waited — one by the fridge, one by the bed. A charcuterie tray and heart-shaped bowl of chocolate-covered strawberries sat on the table. Rose-scented candles were lit throughout the room. Two robes hung near the bathroom.

Romantic. Thoughtful. Over-the-top.

The maid lingered, watching our reactions. The clerk stood beside her with a proud little grin.

"Courtesy of Mr. Witten," they whispered. "Enjoy."

Then they both bowed and gently closed the door behind them.

42

evan/mackenzie

Mac picked up a slice of cheese from the charcuterie tray and surveyed the room like she was casing a getaway route.

"If David was paying me alimony, I'd understand all this effort," she said, eyes narrowing at the trail of rose petals with amused suspicion.

I watched her walk around the bed, stepping over petals like they were sacred. Now that we were here — *alone*, no time limits, no interruptions — I wasn't sure what to lead with. Conversation? Or sex?

When we were younger, the answer was always both. Now, with years of missed chances sitting in the room with us, I hesitated.

"Maybe he just really wants you to be happy?"

"And Grace?"

"Same thing. Maybe we just got lucky with our exes."

I had decided to start with talking.

Mac had other plans.

"That's sweet," she said, already walking toward the bathroom, "but enough talk about *them* for now. I want to get full use of this room. That includes room service — if it's available."

Her shoes came off first. Then, without any fanfare, her dress slid down her body and pooled at her feet.

All that remained was a nude thong and a halter bra — the kind with one hook in the front and *a lot* of promise.

I stared. We'd had sex earlier in the day, but that had been chaotic and rushed. This was different. Now I had time to appreciate the way her body had changed, the strength in her thighs, the way the curve of her ass met the dip of her lower back.

She paused in the doorway and tossed a look over her shoulder.

"You coming to take a shower with me?"

My feet moved before my brain could form a coherent answer.

MacKenzie

The bathroom was warm, the water steaming against the glass of the stall as we stepped inside.

At first, it was gentle — hands gliding over damp skin, suds sliding across shoulders, lips brushing along collarbones. I lathered his chest slowly, working up to his shoulders, his arms, down his back. My fingers traced the places I remembered, the ones I missed.

His skin was smoother than I remembered — but that was part of who Evan was when I met him. Swimmers shaved everything. He used to joke he was more dolphin than man.

When he washed me, he didn't rush. His hands took their time, sliding around my waist and over the curve of my hips. But he didn't linger between my legs — not yet. He was holding back.

"We're doing this in the bed," he said quietly, pressing a kiss to my temple. "I want to take my time with you."

When we stepped out, he wrapped a thick, white towel around me like I was something to protect. As he dried me off, I caught sight of the Poseidon tattoo on his chest — the trident still bold, still sharp, still familiar.

"I dreamed about this," I whispered, tracing it. "How old were you when you got it?"

"Sixteen," he said, leading me to the bed. "My dad signed the form. My mom didn't speak to him for a week. But by eighteen, she actually started to like it."

He grabbed one of the champagne bottles, took a long drink, and passed it to me as he laid back on the bed. I took a sip and set the bottle on the floor.

Then I straddled him — towel sliding off my hips — and let myself take in the full picture. His body. His face. The fact that he was *here*, underneath me, looking up at me like I was the only woman he had ever wanted.

"What about the laser?" I asked, fingers teasing the base of his dick, already thick and hard against his stomach. "That come before or after the tattoo?"

He smirked as I wrapped my hand around him, slowly stroking.

"Before. Chest first. Then the tattoo. But this—" he sucked in a breath as I swirled my thumb over the tip, "—this is *not* playing fair."

I leaned down, trailing kisses along his abs, circling his belly button, dipping lower just to *not* reach where he wanted me most.

"You want fair?" I said. "Or do you want me to make you forget your name?"

His voice cracked. "You put your mouth on me — or your ass. Either one. Right now, I want your ass riding me until you cry. You remember that? I *missed* that..."

I shifted back, my thighs sliding along his hips as I lowered myself down his body. "You're feeling bold because of that bus bathroom. But let's not forget — I made you babble like a man possessed."

I dipped my head toward his dick— but he stopped me with a hand on my arm.

"If you're doing that, I need something to do too. Bring that ass over here."

I arched a brow.

"I bet I can make you cry before you make me forget my profession."

I laughed. "You're on."

I positioned myself over him, knees planted on either side of his chest, hovering just out of reach. I was soaked — I could feel it sliding down my thighs.

"Oh, I *love* this view," he said. "Why are you teasing?"

"I'm multitasking," I murmured. I took a sip of champagne, holding it in my mouth, then dipped my head and took him into my mouth, letting the bubbles roll over his skin as I sucked.

His hips jerked.

At the same time, his mouth found my clit.

The first jolt of pleasure nearly knocked me off balance.

I fought to focus, stroking him with one hand, sliding him deeper into my throat, letting my tongue swirl around the head — all while his tongue flicked against me, slow and deliberate.

"You're holding back," I gasped.

"So are you," he growled. "But not for long."

He slipped two fingers inside me and rubbed my clit with his thumb. My breath caught. I tried to fight it — to win the bet — but he changed the rhythm, alternating suction and pressure until my hips rocked involuntarily.

His free hand gripped my ass, guiding my body lower against his face.

I moaned around his dick. It vibrated through both of us.

That was it. I snapped.

The orgasm hit me like a wave crashing through my chest and hips and spine. I cried out his name, collapsing forward, my body shaking. I was vaguely aware of a tear on my cheek.

Before I could come down from it, Evan flipped me onto my back, hooked my knees, and slid into me with a single, deep thrust.

"Not done yet," he rasped, voice shaking. "I want to *feel* you come again."

His thrusts were hard, controlled, relentless. Each one pushed me higher, made me cling to him tighter. My legs wrapped around his waist. I kissed his neck, his shoulder, his mouth. Everything in me burned for him.

He whispered my name as he came — each syllable dragged out like a prayer.

I felt every pulse of his release inside me.

He collapsed onto my chest. I wrapped my arms around him and held him close, breathless.

Just like old times.

Afterwards, Mac laid her head on my shoulder, one hand resting on my chest like she never left.

"If nothing else," I said, still catching my breath, "we are *excellent* at this."

She laughed softly. I kissed her forehead, then slid my fingers — the same ones I'd had inside her — into my mouth.

"You still taste amazing," I murmured.

She laughed again, nuzzling her face into my neck.

I was already half-hard again, but I didn't want to rush into round two. Not yet. We'd waited years for this. I wanted the *conversation*, too.

"It's been a while," she said quietly. "I hope I've grown. I'm not the same woman you knew. But... I also didn't want to be with anyone else after you."

"You were my first," she added, barely above a whisper.

I looked down at her.

"I *knew* that," I said. "But you never acted unsure. You were bold. You had all these ideas, all this curiosity... you wanted to try everything."

She sat up in bed without bothering to cover herself — something she *never* would have done fifteen years ago. I watched her, amazed at how confidently she moved now. The way her breasts shifted with each motion. Her comfort in her skin. The quiet, grown power of it all.

"I had imagination and no one to try it with," she said. "And then there you were — my real-life romance novel fantasy. A sex god who made me feel seen and safe. You gave me toe-curling, mind-blowing orgasms and actually called me back afterward. I felt lucky. And I trusted the hell out of you. I still do."

I reached for my phone on the nightstand.

"What are you doing?" she asked, finally pulling the sheet over her chest — just enough to tease.

"Sending a group text."

"Excuse me?"

I grinned. "To our exes. Just to say: mission accomplished."

Her eyes went wide. "You're not serious."

"No pictures. Just... a polite update. Maybe they should start a matchmaking service."

"That's *so* weird," she muttered, laughing despite herself. "Are we updating them every time we fuck now? Should we start a group thread?"

I tilted my head. "Tempting."

She leaned over to peek at the message. "Okay, fine. That wasn't as bad as I thought."

"You want it worse, you should've written it," I teased.

She sat up, the sheet dropping again. I couldn't stop staring.

God, I love that.

"So," she said, "did you ever consider working in research? Or for a pharma company? You must've had offers."

"Yeah. Plenty. But we already had Gabe by then, and Grace and I were on the edge. I couldn't give her what she needed... but I could be there for Gabe. I *wanted* to start fresh — just run — but I loved surgery. I loved California."

She nodded, biting her lip.

"Would you move to Miami?" she asked. "Practice here?"

"I've already started the paperwork to get hospital privileges. Wouldn't take much. What about you — if Alex gets in?"

"I've thought about it. Briefly," she said. "But Nashville's been my base for so long..."

"I thought you loved it there?"

"I did. Until after... everything. After us. Then the divorce. I've been surviving more than living."

I watched her for a long moment.

"I'm surprised you're not with someone now. You're beautiful. Brilliant. Funny. Fierce." I paused. "Am I stepping on anyone's toes?"

Her eyes widened. "Of course not. That hasn't changed about me. I wouldn't have let this happen if I was with someone. Not without a phone call first."

She smirked. "Besides, I haven't dated anyone seriously since my divorce."

She laid back and pulled the sheet over her head.

I sat up. "You're serious?"

"Mmhmm."

"What the hell? Same situation we talked about in med school? The whole 'complexity' thing?"

"No," she said, pulling the sheet down again. "This time, it's all on me. I built my life around Alex. There wasn't space for anyone else. And after us — after the divorce — I was convinced I didn't deserve more."

She paused.

"I told myself I was fine. I got used to being alone. But... no one was *you*."

My chest ached.

"The complexity of you not believing you deserve to be happy."

She looked at me. "It's hard to shake. My mom and grandma didn't mean harm. My brother didn't know better. But I still hear them — telling me I was only alive to make sense of other people's deaths. That loving me was dangerous."

Her voice cracked.

"When we were together, I thought I'd outrun that."

"And then I fucked it all up," I said quietly.

The room fell into silence.

I pulled her into my arms.

"You are *enough*," I whispered, over and over, into her skin. Into her hair. Into the ache between us.

She cried, just a little. But when the tears stopped, she let out a breath and rolled over.

"Alright, alright. That's enough. No more tears unless they're orgasm-related."

She padded to the bathroom, then came back and dropped onto the bed beside me.

"What else do you want to know?" she asked.

I turned toward her, drawing lazy circles on her thigh. "Okay, one more question — kind of nosy..."

She smirked. "Go on."

"You always had a high sex drive. How the *hell* have you gone without sex for all this time?"

She grinned. "Two words. Goodie drawer."

Then she reached into her day bag and pulled out a sleek little pink vibrator.

"Okay — that's adorable," I said.

"This guy — and a few of his friends — have come in clutch."

"Cum in clutch?"

"Exactly."

I laughed. "How long have you had that one?"

"I don't know. Why?"

"I just hope you brought more than one," I said, flipping the switch.

43

mackenzie

In the middle of the night, my restlessness pulled Evan out of sleep.

The candles had long since burned out. Moonlight spilled across the bed from the patio window. The sun hadn't risen yet, but we'd have to be back in Miami by one — meaning the bus ride wasn't far off.

"Why are you up already?" Evan murmured, glancing at his watch with a yawn. "I had some ideas about how to spend our last couple of hours..."

He rolled over and began trailing kisses down my neck. By the time his lips closed around my nipple, I could already feel the heat blooming between my legs.

But I couldn't let it happen — not yet. Not until I said what I needed to say.

I gently pulled away and stood up on the bed — *naked* — because if I didn't speak now, I'd lose my nerve.

"Hey! Evan! I want to talk to you."

I bounced once or twice on the mattress, just to make sure I had his full attention.

He propped himself up on one elbow, grinning at me. "All you had to do was *say* something."

He sat up, still chuckling. "Although watching you bounce up and down might not get you the *conversation* you're hoping for."

I glanced at the sheet tented around his hips. Yep. Still had it.

But I held my ground.

"I don't want to be friends with benefits anymore," I blurted out.

Not my smoothest start.

"What do you mean?" He shifted closer. "I didn't think that was even still on the table. I figured we left the 'friends' part behind already."

I shrugged and dropped my gaze. "We haven't said it. We've been having sex, we've been talking, but we haven't actually *said* what we want. And I can't do another situation like before — not without clarity."

Evan reached for my hands. "I think it's pretty damn clear we still love each other — and want to be together."

"But we haven't talked about what comes next. About what happens *after* the sex and the nostalgia and the vacation haze."

He tipped my chin up, meeting my eyes.

"I want *you*. In my life. In my bed. I want to wake up with you, argue about Netflix, fight for the covers. I want to fall asleep on the couch with you and go on trips with you. I want to build the family we always dreamed of — however that looks. I'm not just fucking you because you're hot and this is convenient. It's more than that. It's *always* been more than that."

I felt my heart crack open again — not painfully this time, but gently. Like it had been waiting for this.

"I want that too," I whispered, kissing him. The words tumbled out. "But after our breakup, I convinced myself I wasn't relationship material. If I couldn't make it work with *you*, what chance did I have with anyone else? And then the mess with David... I just shut that part of myself down. I locked the door."

I laughed a little. "But then I saw you again — touched you, talked to you — and I realized I can't *fucking* stand it. My heart is so fucking wide open right now."

Evan smirked. "Your poor patients. You're out here corrupting the children."

"Shut up."

But then I got serious.

"How would this *work*? We live in different cities."

"You mentioned moving to Miami if Alex gets into the Academy, right?"

"Well... yeah. I've thought about it."

"Then let's do it. If our kids both get in, we move here. You open your dream practice, I get hospital privileges, and we figure the rest out together."

He kissed me again. "Just think about it."

"That sounds *amazing*. But what if they *don't* both get in? I can't do another long-distance maybe-we'll-make-it situation."

"Fair. So we make a Plan B."

I looked at him. "Like... would one of us move? Would we pick a whole new city? I don't want caveats. I need to know we're doing this *for real*."

"No caveats," he said softly. "If they don't both get in, we still decide — together. Miami, Nashville, San Francisco, or some new place. Let's each make a list of cities, eliminate the snowy ones — because I'm not shoveling shit — and draw straws if we have to. I can work anywhere. You can, too."

I smiled, tears stinging the corners of my eyes.

"I'm in this for the long haul," he continued. "It's going to be weird, and messy, and wonderful. The kids will need time to adjust. We'll argue. We'll get boring. And sometimes, it'll be wild again. But it'll be *ours*. I married the wrong person because I thought not having you meant I should settle for a friend. But even that didn't work. I don't want to live like that anymore. So — start thinking about your list. We'll talk more when we get back to Miami."

My heart felt like it had grown two sizes. Not in a Hallmark way — in a *this might actually work* kind of way.

Evan gently pushed me back onto the bed, his palm flat against my belly.

"Now — I had started some very important work before you interrupted me. May I continue?"

His fingers slid down my stomach, to my thigh, then in slow circles toward my center.

"Yes, Doctor," I murmured.

His mouth found my breast again. The circles got smaller — more focused. The way he took his time made me arch against the mattress. My fingers knotted in the sheets.

And then all bets were off.

I moaned, loudly — no shame this time — as he wrung another world-shaking orgasm from me with nothing but his mouth, his fingers, and that same determined focus he brought to every surgery.

Afterward, I curled against his chest, completely spent and more content than I'd felt in years.

44

mackenzie

We only slept for two hours — somehow, it was already Thursday.

There was just enough time for a quick dip in the pool, a nod to our med school days. It was the first time in years that we'd been in the water together. I jumped in and started doing laps, determined to make it an actual workout. Evan, of course, tried to turn it into something sweet — arms out, trying to pull me into a hug. I dodged him every time, and soon we were full-on playing keep-away, laughing so loud I'm sure we woke up half the hotel.

Noticing the time, we rushed back upstairs — we had to make it to the pickup point or risk getting stuck here another day. We jumped in the shower — separately — and scrubbed off the chlorine. Thankfully, we'd both taken Grace's advice and packed an extra change of clothes. She'd known we were staying. That had been her warning. We ate whatever breakfast leftovers we could salvage, grabbed my day bag, and hustled downstairs. Evan asked the front desk about the shuttle.

"You're Dr. Robertson, right? Mr. Witten reserved one of the antique cars to take you back to the bus stop," the clerk said.

Evan was thrilled. I took a picture of him standing next to it, and the driver snapped one of us both.

I felt like I was dreaming.

The bus left midmorning. No shenanigans this time — we both slept the entire way back, my head on Evan's shoulder, his arm wrapped around me. When we arrived, Evan texted Grace and David with our arrival time. They were already waiting at the pickup spot.

I expected them to be giddy — lots of "I told you so's" and playful teasing. But David looked... off. Nervous. He wasn't usually like this.

When he hesitated before hugging me, I stepped back. "What's wrong? Is something wrong with Alex?"

"Well...

This man was 6'6" and fidgeting. Not making eye contact. That scared me more than anything.

"What?" My anxiety slammed into me like a truck. My heart jumped. I could feel the sweat start to pool on my lower back, my breath getting shallow.

"Alex —"

I didn't let him finish. Full panic took over. "Is he okay? Why didn't you call me?" I yanked my phone out of my bag. Dead. Completely dead.

I'd been too busy getting fucked five ways 'til Sunday — and something had happened to my kid.

Evan's arm slid around me, steadying me. "It's okay," he murmured. I barely heard him over the chaos in my brain.

"Hang on," David said quickly. "He broke his foot at the pool. Two small bones — some clown—"

"A jealous clown," Grace added, patting my shoulder.

I opened my mouth, but David held up a hand. "Let me finish. Some clown pushed him into the pool. He hit his foot on the side going in. He's in a walking boot for about a month. But — they still want him at the Academy."

David gave a hesitant smile. "Isn't that great?"

"How could you not call me? Or Evan, if my phone was dead? I would have come back!" I couldn't stop myself. The guilt was crawling up my throat like bile.

"Why?" David asked simply.

"I'm his mother!"

"And I'm his father. I was there. He's fine. No tears, no fuss. He even asked me not to call you when he found out where you were."

I blinked. "Why would he do that?"

Had I alienated my own kid?

David shook his head. "You're jumping to the worst-case scenario. He's not mad. If anything, he wanted you to enjoy yourself. He said — his words — *it wasn't a big deal.*"

At least he wasn't angry. But now I felt guilty. He *needed* me, and I wasn't there.

"Stop it." David turned toward the car. "Let's go. You can change at the hotel, then we'll go see your boy — who is doing fine."

Evan stepped in front of me gently. "Mac. Mac."

My thoughts were too loud. I couldn't hear him.

"Samantha MacKenzie."

That snapped me out of it for a second.

"I'm here. Take a breath —"

I saw his face. Beautiful, calm, comforting. He was saying something I couldn't quite hear over the spiraling. I wanted to melt into his arms — but I couldn't. Not now.

He gave me a small push toward the SUV.

I managed a smile — but it didn't reach my eyes.

David dropped Evan and me off at our respective hotels when we arrived at the station, then circled back to pick us up. Grace ran inside to freshen up. I managed to charge my phone a little but still couldn't reach Alex. He was probably already at the pool.

David picked me up first. Probably so we could talk alone.

"I know you're mad," he said once I got in. "I should've called. But I had it under control. And you needed this trip."

"Yes, well, my son being hurt in a pool is important to me. He could've drowned. I wouldn't have been there. This trip was a mistake."

David exhaled. "That's why I didn't tell you. You'd have run back — to do what? Fix it? He was okay. And you and Evan — things looked good. *Relación cercana.* That's good, right?"

"Yeah, but that can't carry into the real world."

"What?"

"I have to be a mother first. I can't worry about myself. I made a promise when I had Alex. I can't be in a relationship and be a mom. It doesn't work."

Even as the words came out, I didn't fully believe them. But they were familiar — almost like I'd already said them in an earlier life.

"So, moms can't have lives?" David asked. "How do you think other women have more than one kid? You're looking for a reason to run."

He pulled up in front of Evan and Grace's hotel.

"Be glad they're getting in the car. We'll talk more when you calm down."

This morning, everything was beautiful.

Now, I was confused. Torn. Scared.

Maybe seeing my kid would help.

Maybe *something* would.

45

evan/mackenzie

Ever since we arrived back in Miami and Mac heard about Alex, she'd been acting differently. I knew what was going through her mind — guilt. Guilt for not putting her son first and foremost at all times, guilt for not being here. Probably some fear too.

I couldn't lose her to this. It felt like our original breakup all over again. I had to talk to her.

When we pulled into the Academy parking lot, there were way more cars than I remembered from Monday or Tuesday. Probably because tomorrow was decision day — the day participants and their parents would find out if they were being invited to extend their stay. A long weekend in Miami didn't hurt either.

I wanted to talk to Mac, but I figured she needed to see Alex first. Make sure he was okay. We could talk later. At least she still held my hand while we walked into the poolside area.

Alex was one of the few swimmers not dressed out. He sat on the bleachers with his booted foot propped on the one in front of him. His whole face lit up when he saw her. He stood — limped, really — and made his way over to give her a hug.

"Hi, Momma! Did you enjoy your trip? I hope you had a good time!" His tone was upbeat, but the side-eye he gave me during the hug was anything but subtle.

I laughed under my breath. I was definitely going to have to talk to him soon.

Mac clutched his shoulders, holding him at arm's length. "Should you be standing on your foot? What did the doctor say? I'm so sorry I wasn't here." The words rushed out of her in one breath.

"It's okay, Momma. Dad was here. I wanted you to enjoy yourself for once. You always do everything for me — I'm okay. Plus, they want me for the year program once my foot heals." He tried to do a one-footed jig, ending with a little flourish.

Mac laughed at his effort, which was a good sign. But I didn't think we were out of the woods just yet.

Grace and I crossed the deck toward Gabe, who was standing with a few of the other boys in his group.

"Hey, son," I said, pulling him in for a quick hug. "Sorry I missed you yesterday."

Gabe grinned. "Mom said you had a date and missed your ride back. That sounds like something I would do!"

I shot Grace a look. "Of course you gave him the version that makes me sound like the dork."

"I call it like I see it. You are a dork," she said without hesitation.

"Yeah, no cap!" Gabe high-fived her.

Grace turned to me, eyes narrowed. "Right on?" she asked, uncertainly.

I smirked. "Back to raiding the stacks, are we? You weren't even alive when that was popular. What, reading old *Jet* magazines again?"

Gabe furrowed his brow. "*Jet* magazine? Is that about planes?"

Grace shook her head and kissed his cheek. "Ignore your father — he's being silly. Go get warmed up. We're gonna watch you swim, then head to Havana Harry's for dinner. A little pre-celebration since tomorrow's the big day. You feeling good?"

"I feel pretty good!" His coach called him over. "Gotta go, Mom and Dad. Love you!"

"Good luck!" we called after him in unison.

Grace turned to me, her voice quieter now. "I just wanted to say I'm sorry again for tricking y'all into staying behind. How did it go?"

I exhaled slowly. "Better than I imagined, at first. We both admitted we want to make this work. But now — I don't know."

Her expression shifted. "I was afraid of that. You need to talk to her now. Before everything you two rebuilt falls apart. Don't let her run."

She tried to ease the moment with a smile. "I'll hold my 'thank you' until after the crisis passes. And the 'I told you so' is on standby."

Normally, I'd laugh. But not this time. I shoved my hands into my pockets. "Grace, she might not even listen. She's different right now. It's like... when we first broke up. That night — I can't do that again."

Grace squeezed my shoulder. "She's just scared. Remember when Gabe broke his arm? I was a whole mess, and I was *there* when it happened. She wasn't. That's heavy. But she'll get through it — you both will. Just don't wait too long to say what needs to be said."

I nodded, but the voice in my head whispered something I didn't want to hear — that it might already be too late.

MacKenzie

Since Alex wasn't swimming, he came up into the bleachers and sat with us to watch Gabe finish his events.

I kept checking on him every few minutes — touching his shoulder, brushing his curls back, asking if he needed water — and even I could tell he was getting tired of me. My irritation with David had started to fade. He still should've called me, but I wasn't as fired up as before.

Evan sat beside me, hand in mine, thumb gently stroking across my skin. I looked at him and remembered Key West — how soft it all felt, how we made plans and finally said the things we needed to say. It was supposed to be our fresh start. But after the injury, I was right back to feeling unsure, scared, overwhelmed.

The whole group seemed to have adopted my mood.

That changed when Alex's coach — the head of his age group — walked over as we started packing up.

"Mr. Witten? Dr. Stephens?" he said.

David's head snapped around to him, and everyone else — Evan, Grace, and Alex — looked at me. I was too deep in my own thoughts, stuffing my goggles and water bottle into my bag.

David tapped my shoulder.

"What?" I snapped, then winced. "Sorry."

"Alex's coach is here."

I turned quickly. "Yes — sorry," I repeated.

The coach just smiled. "No worries. I wanted to congratulate you early. I won't be here for tomorrow's ceremony, but Alex is being invited to the full-year program. We'll get started once his foot heals. You two will still need to fill out some paperwork before you leave, so you'll be called to the conference room tomorrow."

He extended a hand to Alex. "Congratulations, young man. I see great things ahead for you."

Alex looked like he could float out of the building, boot and all.

The coach turned to Evan and Grace next. "Your son's coach was looking for you too. I'm sure he'll be by in a minute."

Before we left campus, David pulled out his phone and made a reservation at Havana Harry's.

"I think I'm just gonna go back to the hotel," I muttered. "I have a headache."

"Still mad? Or just looking for the right moment to kick my ass?" he teased.

"Oh, I *would* kick your ass if I could. I'm just biding my time. Gotta catch you off guard."

He grinned. "Your head probably hurts from stressing too hard. You're raising your blood pressure when you should be enjoying your damn vacation — or planning your future."

"Easy for *you* to say. I'm trying to accept that it was okay for you to take care of our kid. I know that in my *head* — but my heart isn't there yet."

"I get it. Which is why you need your own life too. Alex is going to leave *both* of us," he said, pointing at me and then himself. "We've gotta be able to stand on our own. He's gonna move away — are you planning to move to Miami if he gets in? Especially now?"

"I was. I'd been thinking about it. But now... I don't know. I feel overloaded. What about you?"

"I'm considering it too. But here's the real question — is Evan?"

I flinched. Walked right into that one.

"He says he is. Yesterday, we said we'd move together," I mumbled. "And don't say it."

I didn't need the speech. Didn't need him to tell me that if Evan and I moved to Miami together, it could all work. I already knew it wasn't that simple.

46

mackenzie/evan

Unsurprisingly, the boys were boisterous at dinner, and Grace did her best to hold up the adult end of the conversation — though she had to work for it.

My headache had faded, and I wasn't mad at David anymore. But I was uneasy — restless in my skin — when it came to Evan. I barely spoke, and when I did, my answers came in flat little syllables.

Evan tried to talk to me, tried to pull me out of whatever spiral I was in. But I wanted to cry every time he looked at me. I wanted to enjoy being here, to hold on to what we had in Key West — but the dream had deflated. Of course my life wouldn't get to be *that* good.

I'd just proven I couldn't balance motherhood and a relationship. I'd forgotten my responsibilities, and for what? Sex and fantasy. It was selfish. And maybe I wasn't built for anything more than showing up for my son. Maybe that was all I was supposed to do.

David was starting to get annoyed. I was snappy with him even though he didn't deserve it. He'd done nothing wrong — he was Alex's father, and I trusted him. But I wasn't going to say that. Not tonight.

Eventually, even Grace had enough. She threw up her hands, clearly done trying. By then, we were all eating in silence.

The boys didn't seem to notice. They were deep in their own conversations, probably wondering why all the grown-ups were acting weird.

I couldn't wait to leave.

While we waited outside for our Lyfts — one SUV and one Accord — Evan gently tugged me to the side.

"What's going on with you?" he asked, eyes searching mine. "Last night and this morning, we were planning our future. Now you won't even look at me. Are you regretting it? I thought we agreed — no matter what happened with our kids, we'd figure it out. We'd start our lives together."

I blinked, startled by how raw he sounded. "No. Not really. I *want* us to try. But —"

"But?" His voice tightened. "But what?"

"What about our kids?" I whispered. "I just proved I don't have the capacity to juggle this. I forgot what I was supposed to be doing. And Alex... he already tried to fight you once. What if he's not okay with any of this?" I looked down. "I don't know what I'm doing, Evan."

Evan

My mouth fell open. "What the hell, Mac..."

I was stunned. Just like when she'd walked out years ago — that night we fought about Christine and our residencies. But this? This was *so* Mac. That instinct to self-sabotage before anyone else could beat her to it. That deep-rooted belief that she wasn't allowed to have good things.

"My son got hurt, and I wasn't there. I'm out here making promises without really thinking about him."

"It wasn't your fault," I said firmly. "And David *was* there. Alex wasn't alone. And he doesn't want you to be either."

She shook her head. "It's my job to be there. I'm a parent first."

"You can be a parent *and* still have a life, Mac. You deserve one. Hell — I know your son wants that for you."

"He's a *child*," she snapped.

I stepped in, eyes locked on hers. "And what happens when he's not? When he goes to college, or the Olympics, or gets married? What then? You gonna sit in silence waiting on a text message or a holiday visit while everyone else moves forward?"

She looked down, jaw tight.

"What happens if this doesn't work out?" she said. "What if he gets caught in the crossfire?" Her voice trembled. "I'm his mother. That has to come first."

I reached out and gently took her arm, guiding her closer.

"What about what *you* want? What you *need*?" I placed my hand on her chest, feeling her heart race beneath my palm. I stepped in until our noses almost touched. Her lips parted. Her breath caught.

"You know if I kissed you right now, you'd fall apart in my hands," I whispered. "You can't look at me like this and pretend you don't want us."

Her chest rose, then fell — slow, shaky, like she was trying not to give in.

She tried to back away, but I didn't let go. Not yet.

"You're searching for a reason to run. Again. Back then it was my schedule, Christine, whatever excuse made it easier to leave. Now it's Alex. But this time?" I leaned in. "I'm not letting you give up on us. Not without a fight."

She opened her mouth. "Evan —"

God, her voice. I wasn't trying to escalate this. I just wanted her to *see* what we could be. But I'd gone too far. I was hard as hell and barely hanging on.

I checked my phone. *Where the hell is that damn ride share?*

Alex wanted to ride with Gabe — the two of them were buzzing about the idea of becoming roommates if Gabe got in too. David and Grace, wisely, gave us space. They got into the SUV with the boys.

When the Accord pulled up, Mac and I climbed in quickly.

As soon as the door closed, I reached under her dress and caressed her inner thigh. Her breath hitched. She shifted her hips, trying to guide my hand higher — closer to where she wanted me.

I let her inch me there. Almost. But not quite.

She was soaked. That didn't help my self-control.

"Please," she whispered.

I leaned into her ear. "And you're ready to give *this* up again?" I said, my voice a groan. "You think this only hurts you?"

I'd waited fifteen years for her.

She wasn't going to take this from us.

But first, we needed to fuck.

47

david

The four of us climbed into the SUV, leaving the drama behind — or so we thought.

But the tension had followed us.

This should've been a night to celebrate — one of the boys officially accepted into the Academy, the other waiting hopefully. Instead, we were wrapped in silence, weighed down by Mac's unraveling and the domino effect it had on all of us.

Grace and I took the middle row. The boys sat behind us, still riding their high from earlier.

Grace gave me a long side-eye. "What the hell was that dinner? I felt like I was babysitting grown-ass adults. The teenagers had better manners."

I exhaled, pinching the bridge of my nose. "It's Mac. Still mad at me — still freaked out about Evan. She's spiraling, and she doesn't want to talk to anybody. She probably needs to get laid again. Might help her see straight."

Grace rolled her eyes. "I think the sex is what *threw* her off. From the sound of it, she's been very well handled these past two days."

I laughed in spite of myself. "You might be right. But it's the aftermath. She's thinking too far ahead — worst-case scenario mode. Childhood stuff, maybe. She's always waiting for the other shoe to drop. I think she wants to talk to Alex first before she really commits to anything."

Grace nodded slowly. "That makes sense. Still — what do we do in the meantime? I'm worried. Not just for her. If this blows up, we could lose *everything*. The whole group falls apart. Evan's already hanging on by a thread."

I leaned back against the seat. "If I could, I'd lock her in a damn hotel room until she calms down. But we've got one advantage — she can't leave without Alex. And we know exactly where he'll be for the rest of the weekend." I shrugged. "So there's that."

Grace winced. "Shit. I might've made it worse."

I turned to her, eyebrow raised. "What do you mean?"

She looked down at her lap. "Evan's family is coming tomorrow. His mom, his sister, her husband — even his grandmother. They used to visit him at the Academy, and I thought it'd be nice for Gabe. I didn't think about... *all* this."

"Wait — what?!"

"I know. I know," she said quickly. "I invited them before all this started. And now I'm afraid it's going to make everything ten times worse. I was just trying to do something thoughtful."

I ran my hand over my face. "So, we can't stop the visit. Which means we've got to manage *her*."

Grace gave a dry laugh. "And how exactly do we pull that off?"

"We keep reminding her she deserves this. That it's okay to be happy. Get her to talk to Evan — and to Alex. Let them *all* speak their peace." I paused. "I'll talk to her in the morning. Try to get through."

Grace nodded. "Yeah. It's not just about her anymore. If she falls apart, we all do. I'm honestly scared about what happens next."

48

evan

Our Lyft driver was definitely ready for us to *get out of his car*. Between the tension, the not-so-subtle touches, and the way Mac kept adjusting her seat like I wasn't three seconds from losing my mind, the man couldn't hit "end ride" fast enough.

We'd barely made it to the curb at her hotel before Mac grabbed my hand and started speed-walking toward the lobby like she was on a mission. In the elevator — once she was sure we were alone — she shoved me against the wall and slid her hand down the front of my pants.

"This is payback for the car," she said, voice low and smug as her hand found what she was looking for. "O-h-h-h." She smirked. "I'm going to enjoy this." Then she pulled out her room key and pressed it into my hand. "Be a gentleman and open the door."

The second it clicked open, she shoved me inside and kicked it shut behind us. She was all over me — pulling at my shorts, pushing me backward. I had every intention of taking control tonight, but it was clear she had her own agenda.

My shorts dropped to my ankles, and I didn't even have time to step out of them before she was on her knees. I opened my mouth to say something — anything — but I couldn't remember a single word in the English language.

She took her time. Not just teasing — *ruining* me. I knew I wasn't going to last long like this, and just when I thought I'd lose it right there standing in the middle of the room, she pulled back.

"You thought I was gonna make it that easy?" she said, getting to her feet and wiping her mouth with the back of her hand. "You weren't playing fair earlier. Two can play that game."

I squinted at her, catching my breath. "That's fucked up."

She smirked. "On the couch. Now."

She stripped off her thong, hiked up her dress, and stalked over like she owned the room. I shuffled to the couch, nearly tripping on my damn shorts, and fell back just in time for her to straddle my thighs.

She didn't sink down. Just hovered. Letting the tip of my dick graze her while she kept eye contact.

"You're gonna wait. Because I'm in control tonight," she said, hips shifting just enough to make me twitch. "And you're gonna do what I say — until I say otherwise."

I reached for her sundress straps, pulling them down and revealing the clasp on her bra. "I like where this is going."

"Good," she whispered. "But don't get ahead of yourself."

I popped the clasp and her breasts spilled free. I took one in my mouth, teasing her nipple while her hips rolled just enough to brush her clit against me. Over and over — just enough to keep us both teetering.

"I thought you were in control," I said, voice rough. "You're doing everything without me."

When she got close, I shifted just enough to throw her off. She hissed, biting her lip.

"You didn't follow instructions," she snapped. "I didn't say stop."

"Frustrated?" I grinned. "Guess that makes two of us."

Wrong move.

She leaned over, grabbed her purse off the couch, and pulled out a box.

"What's that?" I asked, narrowing my eyes.

"Something new," she said sweetly, sliding a double ring contraption with a rose on it out of the package. "Amazon's fast. Figured we might need a little... motivation."

She slipped one ring around the base of my dick. I nearly groaned.

Then she positioned the rose against her clit, and lowered herself onto me — slow, tight, and dripping. I felt the vibration kick in as she buried me inside her... then didn't move.

"And if you move," she said, eyes dangerous, "I'm getting up. You didn't make me come. You didn't beg. You wanted to play, so let's *play*."

I lasted maybe three minutes.

Begged like my life depended on it.

She won. And I didn't even care.

When we were done, Mac slid off my lap and curled up beside me on the couch, legs tucked under her, breathing steady but quiet.

I didn't say anything right away. She'd needed this — the control, the choice, the *power*. I just wasn't sure if it made her feel any better about what was going on in her head.

Eventually, I reached for her hand. "Let's get in bed."

She nodded, and we crawled under the covers without a word.

For a while, we just laid there — staring at each other, soft in the dark, skin still humming.

"You're so beautiful," I said, fingers lacing with hers.

She shook her head. "You're just being sweet. I'm okay. I never really got why you even came up to me in the first place. What's that phrase — 'Men don't make passes at girls who wear glasses'?"

"You were beautiful then too."

"I always thought you were into my boobs."

I shrugged. "Not gonna lie — I *definitely* noticed them. But there was something else. I just... I wanted to know you."

She nudged my shoulder with her knuckle, then went quiet again. It felt like we were floating between something real and something that could slip through our fingers if we weren't careful.

"I know you're scared," I said finally. "Scared you can't juggle being a mom and being in a relationship. That we'll mess this up again. That Alex'll get hurt."

She didn't answer.

"You don't think I'm scared too?" I asked. "I'm trusting that we love each other enough to figure this out. That we can actually build something this time."

"I don't know," she said softly.

"How about this," I offered. "Let's just... enjoy this weekend. The parties. Dinner. Time together. No pressure. And then we figure out what comes next — together."

She groaned. "I haven't even talked to Alex yet."

"It's not fifteen years ago. We're older. Smarter. Sexier. We can make Mac and Evan whatever the hell we want Mac and Evan to be. I'm just saying."

She didn't respond. She just pressed her face into my chest, nose grazing the ink over my heart.

"I really do love you," she mumbled.

I pulled her closer and held on.

Neither of us said another word before we drifted off to sleep.

49

evan/mackenzie

I woke up first.

Mac was tucked under my arm, breathing slow and even, her hair fanned across my chest. She'd finally slept soundly after a restless night, so I figured I'd sneak in a quick swim before our breakfast with the exes.

But the second I tried to slide my arm out from under her, she stirred.

"Where you going?" she asked, voice thick with sleep as she pushed up onto one elbow. The sheet slipped down, baring just enough to make it hard as hell to think straight.

"I was gonna hit the pool. Thought I could get out without waking you."

She grinned, slow and devilish. "I do wanna come... but not in the pool."

She scooted to the edge of the bed, legs bare, eyes locked on mine. If I'd been *really* committed to swimming, that would've been my cue to leave.

Spoiler: I didn't move.

Within seconds, she had her legs wrapped around me and I was back in the bed like I'd never tried to leave.

"I'll go with you *after* you get me off in nine minutes," she whispered, tapping her watch. "Fast and dirty. We've got a deadline. You in?"

Was that even a question?

It was everything she promised — hot, playful, filthy. No teasing. No build-up. Just sweat and skin and a countdown that made it feel even hotter.

I beat the clock, but swimming was officially off the agenda.

Afterward, as we lay tangled together, I thought about how easily we'd slipped back into rhythm. It had only been five days — five — since she'd come back into my life, and somehow it already felt like we'd never left.

The sex. The chemistry. The avoidance.

Old patterns, like muscle memory.

But that last one — the slow-walking of hard conversations — that's the part that got us in trouble before. If we wanted this to actually work, we'd have to break that cycle for good.

Mackenzie

He was out cold beside me, one arm draped over my waist, breath warm on my neck.

He'd earned the nap. I'd given him a challenge, and he passed with flying colors.

But I wasn't sleeping. Not anymore.

I kept replaying our conversation from the night before. If we were serious about trying again — *really* trying — I had to talk to Alex. A real, honest, no-fluff conversation. Not just about Evan being in town, but about what it would mean if Evan were in our lives for good.

Alex was still little when his dad and I divorced. He didn't remember what it felt like to have two parents under one roof. And lately, he'd been acting like he was on high alert anytime Evan and I got too close.

That worried me.

But I was the adult here. I couldn't let fear dictate my future — or his. I had the right to be happy. And if Evan was part of that happiness, then I had to handle things like a grown-ass woman.

The longer I sat with that thought, the calmer I felt. Like I had a little more control. Like maybe I *could* figure this out.

Then Evan's phone buzzed at 7:30.

He groaned, reaching under my head for it. When he read the screen, he gasped.

"What?" I asked. "Who is it?"

"My mother," he said, sitting up straighter. "She's at the airport. With Liza. And Stephon. And *the baby*. And my grandmother. What the hell are they doing in Miami?"

Right on cue, *my* phone buzzed.

I opened the text and groaned. "Ree's on her way too. She lands at noon."

We looked at each other.

"You invite anyone?" I asked.

He shook his head. "Nope. You?"

"Not a soul."

We both paused, same thought clicking into place.

"Grace," we said at the same time.

He sighed. "Yeah... probably Grace. But don't worry. My family's gonna be happy to see you."

I tried to act cool while typing a quick update to Ree, knowing full well she wouldn't see it until after she landed. I felt Evan press a kiss to my cheek before getting up to make coffee. A normal thing. A boyfriend thing.

I didn't let myself look at him while he moved around the room. If I did, I'd fall back in, heart first.

And I couldn't do that. Not yet.

I needed time. Space. A real decision.

But maybe I could still enjoy the process while I figured it out.

By the time we had coffee in hand, Grace called. Evan put her on speaker.

"I see you got the texts!" she chirped, entirely too cheerful. "Isn't it exciting?"

"You gave them the details, didn't you?" Evan asked.

"Of course I did. Everyone's coming to support the boys — and maybe... celebrate something else?" she asked with a knowing lilt.

"No news on this front," I said quickly.

"Yet," Evan added.

I cut him a look, but he grinned and hung up.

"Why are you giving her false hope?" I asked.

"Because I don't think it's false." He reached for my hands. "You're here. You spent the night. You initiated sex *multiple times.* You fell asleep on my chest. That doesn't scream *I'm done with you.*"

"Evan..."

"I'm not gonna be passive this time. You know I love you. You know we work — emotionally, sexually, everything. We don't have to plan a wedding tomorrow. Hell, we don't even have to live together. But we could try. Move to Miami. Take it slow. See what this could be."

He squeezed my hands, voice soft.

"Just... think about what it would feel like to be loved — *really* loved — every day. To have someone protect your heart, your mind, your soul. I swear to you, I will."

Then he lifted my hand to his lips and kissed the back of it. "We're Mac and Evan Part 2: Electric Boogaloo."

I couldn't help the smile. "That sounds about right."

We met Grace, David, and the boys for breakfast at a cozy spot near the Academy. David had already scooped the boys up for a morning outing before their afternoon swim coach evaluations. We'd all head back to campus together later.

They were practically bouncing in their seats with excitement — and eating like they were prepping for hibernation. David and Evan tried to keep up. Grace and I just watched, sipping coffee, trying to stay in the moment.

I woke up feeling calm.

But by the time we got to the café, that calm was unraveling.

While we waited for our food, David leaned over and asked if I could step outside for a sec. He was sitting against the wall, so the whole booth had to shift to let us out. He held the door for me, then turned, straight to the point.

"You gonna talk to Alex today?"

I narrowed my eyes.

"It's Friday. There's still this weird fog hanging over everybody. It was over dinner last night too…"

That set me off.

"It's my life," I snapped, louder than I meant to. "You're acting like I'm picking a side dish."

He didn't flinch. "It *could* be that easy, if you let it. You've been through some heavy shit. No one's denying that. But you don't have to turn your life into the martyrdom Olympics."

My jaw dropped. "Excuse me?"

"I'm sorry, but damn — you're killing the vacation vibe. You're killing *me*. Grace and I thought you and Evan would reconnect and we'd have something real to celebrate. Now I'm starting to wonder if we should've even gotten involved. If you *want* to be happy."

"Oh, so you *were* meddling."

"That's what you took from what I said? Just… talk to Alex. Decide. Please."

He walked back inside without another word.

I stayed on the sidewalk, staring through the window.

Everyone inside looked like they were doing just fine. Laughing. Eating. Moving on.

Why did this decision feel like such an impossible weight to *me*?

After we finished eating, Grace dropped one more surprise. She told the boys that Evan's whole family was flying in — and that one of *my* friends was coming too. Gabe lit up. Even Alex seemed excited, probably feeding off his friend's energy.

And that's when it hit me.

Alex had never really had family. Not in the way Gabe did. No visits. No reunions. No warm arms or doting grandparents or aunts who snuck him extra dessert.

Had I already failed him in that way?

I felt the guilt punch me right in the chest. And still, under all that mess in my head... I was excited to see Evan's family again.

His mother, Miss Lorraine. His sister, Liza. They were the first people who made me feel like I *belonged* to something.

I met them at the hospital after I nearly drowned. Evan was taken in as a precaution, and they rushed in to make sure he was okay — then never left my side. Miss Lorraine hovered over me like she already knew I was family. Liza folded me in too, like I was someone worth knowing.

They loved me before Evan even said the words.

And when we fell apart, I cut myself off from them completely.

Maybe they'd still be happy to see me. Maybe not.

But there was a time — a real, solid time — when being around them reminded me what it felt like to *be wanted*.

And even if I didn't know where Evan and I were going next... part of me still wanted to feel that again.

50

evan/mackenzie

Walking into the Academy conference room that afternoon, Grace and I were both anxious about the verdict from Gabe's coaches. She was visibly more tense than I was—fidgeting in her seat and running her fingers through her hair. Gabe sat at the end of the table, hands in his lap, head down. His earbuds were in, probably playing some kind of positive affirmation loop.

"Don't worry," I whispered, more for myself than her. "No matter what, it's a win-win. He's young. We can always come back and try again."

Grace rolled her eyes. Even for her, my overly sunny optimism had limits. "I know. I know. I just really want this for him. This whole week has been stressful—in more ways than one."

Right on time, at 12:30, four coaches and assistants filed into the room, led by the head swim coach. Gabe pulled out his earbuds, sitting up a little straighter.

"Good afternoon!" the head coach said, reaching across the table to shake our hands. "Glad to see all of you here."

We greeted him in return.

"I'm happy to officially welcome Gabe to our developmental program." He smiled at Gabe. "It's a one-year program—we can discuss the exact start date later—with options to extend depending on development and interest."

Gabe jumped up and shouted, "Yes-s-s!" then hugged Grace and me tight. His grin stretched ear to ear.

The other coaches offered their congratulations. I didn't want to hang around much longer—I was itching to get back to the hotel, where my family was due any minute. We could talk logistics later. What mattered was that Gabe made it in. He'd done it.

The head coach made small talk for a few more minutes and asked me about my own time at the Academy. I smiled through it, but I could practically hear my family groaning from a distance. Nobody wanted to rehash my Olympic hopeful days right now.

Eventually, I steered the conversation to a close. We thanked the coaches again, then headed out.

MacKenzie

Alex's meeting was scheduled twenty minutes after Gabe's, so we crossed paths with them in the hallway just after they left the conference room. The second I heard Gabe had made it in, I threw my arms around him.

"I'm so proud of you!" I said, then held him at arm's length and hugged him again. "You're going to kill it this year. I'll be able to say I knew you back when."

He grinned at me and then, very casually, asked, "Are you going to be my stepmom?"

I kept smiling—barely. "Heh... I... hmm... yeah. I'm so proud of you!" What the hell. That was the third person this morning to press me on this.

I pivoted, hugging Grace next and then Evan. His hug lingered.

"Congratulations," I said softly. "I knew Gabe would make it through the gauntlet this week."

"Thanks," he said, pulling back to look at me. "He and Alex can start planning their dorm layout."

He studied me. "How are you doing? I saw your argument with David this morning."

I took a breath. "I don't want to talk about it. But I do want to tell you something."

I hesitated, fingers fidgeting with the hem of my dress. "I miss you. It's only been a few hours, and I already miss being next to you. I bet that makes you happy."

One of my braids had slipped from the loose bun I threw together this morning. I left it hanging.

"You know it does," he said. "Proves my point." His voice softened. "My family's back at the hotel. I might bring them by later—they want to see the Academy again. But after your meeting, come to my room. We'll have cocktails with the family. They're dying to see you."

I nodded, heart thudding. I wasn't sure if it was nerves, excitement, or both.

Once the Robertsons cleared out, we stepped into the conference room for Alex's verdict. Even though I technically knew he was in, I still had butterflies. Until it was in writing, I couldn't relax.

And then... there was Evan.

I wasn't as angry anymore about what happened with Alex's injury. Not really. But I still wasn't sure if it was fair to drag my son through the emotional rollercoaster of a rekindled romance. What if Evan and I didn't work out?

I dropped my head down on the table. Maybe if I stayed like this, the questions would stop.

David, now calm and low-key again, sat beside Alex. "Hey," he said gently. "Sorry about this morning. Have you made a decision yet?"

He tucked the loose braid back into my bun and gave me a soft pat on the back.

"He's fine," I said, still talking into the table. "It's my issue. I've been living one way for so long, and now I'm being shown a different path. One that might actually be better."

"You didn't have to be alone all this time," David murmured. "Who told you that was the only way?"

Alex listened to our conversation like we were speaking a language he'd never heard.

"I thought you and Dr. Evan were getting back together," he said suddenly. "I was kinda excited about having a brother."

Even my thirteen-year-old thought it was simple. Why didn't I?

"Let's talk about that after we get your results," I said, still face-down.

Alex shrugged and propped his boot up on a chair. "You always tell me to go after what I want. That's what I'm doing. Why can't you?"

Damn.

The coaches entered the room. I lifted my head and sat up straight. Time to look like a functioning adult.

The department head repeated the same language from Gabe's meeting. "Alex, we're looking forward to seeing your development in our program. You've shown great promise. Depending on your progress, there may be options to extend."

Alex and David jumped in with questions, and I just sat there, heart full. I was so proud of my son. So damn proud.

When we finally escaped the meeting, we found Grace and Gabe waiting.

Alex strutted out of the building like a champion, chest puffed out, arms wide. Gabe ran to him, and they performed their little victory handshake like they'd been waiting all week for this moment.

Grace hugged me. "Congrats," she said. Then she pulled back and searched my eyes. "I know things are complicated right now. But just... follow your heart. That's all I'll say."

We waited around for the Academy's celebratory ceremony. Evan had called earlier to confirm that his family would be meeting us after freshening up. Of course, Liza wanted to get the baby cleaned up, and his mom and grandmother probably needed a few minutes to catch their breath.

I paced a bit, nerves kicking in. It had been years since I'd seen them. Years since I vanished from their lives after Evan and I fell apart.

What if they hadn't forgiven me?

I didn't think I had it in me to survive another emotional ambush today.

51

mackenzie/evan

Once the Academy head notified all participants of their status — some were recommended to other training programs or encouraged to keep developing and try again later. Others received invitations to a shorter session with possible extensions. There were options for aspiring swimmers at all levels.

We were just glad our sons got the most coveted one.

The ceremony started right at 3 p.m. There were a few speeches from the Academy head and select coaches. A couple of the current students walked around with trays of champagne or apple juice for the guests.

Grace and I took a glass of champagne and made sure our sons had the apple juice. No underage drunken scenes on our watch. A little annoyed by our attentiveness, both boys made excuses to go find their friends.

"Should we keep an eye on them?" I joked.

"Maybe. Nah — you don't think they'd sneak champagne, do you?"

The young woman Addy — the one who flirted with Alex on the first day — overheard us as she passed by with a tray of drinks. She remembered me and stopped to chat.

"Hi! Mrs. Stephens, I'm glad you're still here. I guess that means Alex got into the extended program?" She leaned closer with a conspiratorial grin. "I figured. He's got the perfect swimming build. If he gets his height from his father, he definitely has potential. I'm calling it now." She winked, handed me another glass, and kept walking.

I toasted her, trying not to laugh, as Grace grabbed a second glass off the tray with a grimace. She muttered, "Thanks for my glass," under her breath.

The hair on my neck stood up right before I felt Evan behind me.

"I'm back."

I spun to face him — way too glad to see him again. But before I could say anything, I saw them. His mother Lorraine. His grandmother Rosemary. His sister Liza and brother-in-law Stephon. And in Stephon's arms, their one-month-old daughter, Eliana.

I gave Evan a quick hug, then walked toward his mother. Liza and Stephon stayed with Evan, who kept a careful eye on me while I spoke to Miss Lorraine.

She looked amazing. Older, sure — her hair was fully gray now, pulled back in a neat clasp — but still slim, spry, and unmistakably regal. The moment I got close enough, she hugged me tightly.

"Oh my. You're still beautiful," she said, stepping back with a bright smile. "MacKenzie! It's been so long." She pulled me into another hug. "You're a pediatrician, right?"

"I am. It's good to see you, Miss Lorraine. You look wonderful."

"I'm getting old, but I'm doing fine." She glanced around. "I've heard a lot about your son. Where is he?"

"He's somewhere around here! I'll definitely introduce you tonight. He and Gabe have grown really close this week — you'll be tired of seeing them together."

"They're acting like brothers already," she said with a nudge. "And you're still in Tennessee?"

I skipped over the first comment and answered the second. "Yes, ma'am. Still there."

"For now, right? Are you moving down here with your son? I remember how hard it was sending Evan off back then. He didn't care — but I did."

"I don't know. We just found out Alex was accepted a few hours ago. There's a lot to decide."

"Does my son play a role in those decisions?" she asked, blunt as ever, her eyes twinkling.

I frowned. Evan had clearly given her a heads up. I didn't have an answer for her — and I wasn't about to talk through our mess with his mother. Thankfully, Liza, Stephon, and Evan came over before I had to.

It had been years, but seeing Liza again hit me like a wave. She was shorter than me, all ballerina posture and soft new-mom curves. Stephon had filled out, too — not as muscular as before, but still solid and happy.

I was happy for them. I wondered if I'd ever feel that settled.

"MacKenzie!" Liza hugged me tight. "I wish we had stayed in touch! It's so good to see you."

"I know." For a second, I felt like I was going to cry. So much wasted time. I blinked fast and pulled back. "Let's skip to the good part. Can I meet the baby?"

Stephon teased, "It's been a while. You ready?"

"You haven't lost your sense of humor," I said, smiling as I held out my arms. "It's good to see you, Stephon."

He placed Eliana in my arms, and the moment she settled in, something in me softened. She gurgled and waved her tiny hands. She had Liza's eyes and the sweetest lashes. I cooed — she cooed back. Perfect.

And then it hit me. A twinge in my chest. I'd loved Alex's babyhood as much as I could — but I was a resident, stressed and sleepless, with a husband who picked up the slack. There were moments I missed. Holding this baby brought them all back.

While I made faces at Eliana, I could feel Evan watching me. I didn't turn around. I didn't need to.

I knew exactly what he was thinking — about what it would mean if we ever had a child together. I hadn't thought about having another baby in years. But in that moment, I was... baby-curious.

I handed Eliana back with a little sigh, and Lorraine immediately began fussing over her granddaughter.

"Are your ovaries hurting?" Liza teased. "Suddenly want one of your own?"

"Honestly? A little." I smiled. "It's been a long time since I held a baby who wasn't a patient."

"We've got a lot of catching up to do," Liza said, wrapping an arm around my shoulders. "I should've kept in touch — no matter what happened between you and Evan."

Stephon shifted the baby to his shoulder and turned her toward us. She had her eyes open now, staring toward Liza. I happened to be in the way, but for a second, it felt like she was looking straight at me.

Miss Rosemary came over with a walker, Gabe and Alex trailing behind her. Evan helped his grandmother into a chair, then drifted back toward his mom. But his eyes stayed on me.

"Well, here's my baby!" I said as Alex walked up. I beamed at everyone. "This is Alexander Stephens Witten — future Olympic hopeful, coming soon to a pool near you."

"Momma! I'm not a baby." But he didn't pull away when I wrapped my arm around him.

I introduced him to everyone — even Eliana. To my surprise, he was interested. He'd never been around babies much, but something about her drew him in. He and Gabe took turns playing peek-a-boo.

Miss Rosemary asked Alex a few questions, and he immediately stopped playing and gave her his full attention. I was proud. David and I had done something right there.

Evan tapped my shoulder and pointed at the baby.

I gave him a look. "Really?" I hissed.

He just grinned. "You know we haven't been careful the last few days —"

I shot him a glare as he walked over and picked up his niece. That killer smile again. He wasn't wrong, though.

We were both doctors. You'd think we'd have discussed birth control before jumping into bed — but nope. I wasn't that worried. I was regular and probably in the safe zone. Still, I mentally kicked myself. Just another thing to think about.

David emerged from the crowd holding a water bottle. He paused to look at the baby but aimed his comments at me.

"I had a few more questions for the staff and took another call. Would've brought you, but you looked busy. Introduce me to your in-laws?"

I grunted but did the honors. The grandmothers lit up — as grandmothers do — and David lapped it up. Smooth answers, some in Spanish, all charm.

By the end, they were in love with him. Even Liza was grinning, which made Stephon frown.

I noticed Grace was missing — probably by design. Being polite to ex-in-laws was enough. In the middle of it all, another tap on my arm distracted me from my thoughts.

"Ree!" I squealed.

We hugged like teens.

Ree had grown her locs out and tipped them blonde. She was still fit — running several times a week despite her hectic NICU schedule.

"Girl! It's been forever. Since that Chicago convention, right?" she said. "You look amazing!"

"So do you. Love the glasses." I stepped back. "How's neonatology treating you?"

"I'm just glad to be around people over ten pounds." She grinned. "Anyway, Alex is my de facto godson. He's not a baby anymore, but man — handsome! You had to have started fighting girls off already."

"Starting," I muttered.

"Where's Evan? This is his whole family, right? I think I met his mom and sister once in Nashville."

I introduced her to everyone. Evan came over to hug her and talk shit.

Evan

Mac got pulled into a conversation with my mom and grandmother, so I ended up chatting with Ree.

"You haven't settled down yet?" I asked.

"I blinked and realized I missed the deadline. Now I'm trying to catch up."

I laughed. "You're not the only one."

She narrowed her eyes. "Okay, so what's the deal with you and Mac?"

"No deal. We're just... enjoying the time."

Ree rolled her eyes. "That's the lie you're going with?"

I shrugged. "We're in a good place."

"You two are exhausting." She sipped her drink. "Y'all were so cute in med school. I thought by now you'd be married with teenagers."

I didn't answer.

"Don't blow it this time," she said.

As the party wound down, I walked up behind Mac and wrapped my arms around her. For a moment, she relaxed against me.

Then she pulled away.

"Can we talk?" I asked. "Somewhere quiet?"

She nodded. We stepped out toward the pool.

"You coming back to my room tonight?" I asked gently. "This week has been everything. Yeah, it hasn't been perfect — but the problem wasn't even us this time."

She looked down. "I think you need to be with your family tonight. I'm still thinking. I need to talk to Alex tomorrow. Don't rush me."

I exhaled hard. "Mac... I think you get off on this."

She blinked. "What?"

"Being self-sacrificing. Like you don't believe you deserve to be happy."

"What the hell? How dare you?"

"Am I wrong?"

"Not now. I don't want to do this now."

"Then when?" I stepped closer. "I'd burn it all down for you — give me something."

MacKenzie

I didn't say anything. Because he wasn't wrong.

But I felt frozen. Like if I said the wrong thing, I'd lose it all.

And so, I said nothing. Did nothing.

He tilted my chin up. "I can't believe we're here again. You're shutting me out. You think you don't deserve happiness — because of what your parents gave up for you."

I pulled away. That was low. And true.

"I almost broke through that — we almost did. Twice. I'm fighting for your happiness more than you are." He shook his head. "Maybe I should let you fight your demons alone."

I stared at him. I could see it. The frustration. The truth.

"Thanks for telling me that," I said, voice low. "Be grateful. You don't have to deal with me or my demons anymore."

I turned on my heel and walked off before he could see me cry.

I ducked into the nearest restroom to pull myself together. I think I just broke up with Evan.

Again.

I called David.

He answered on the first ring. "Where are you? Evan's looking for you — he's pissed."

"I fucked it up," I whispered. "I fucked it all up. Just... make sure Alex gets where he needs to go. I'll see you tomorrow."

Then I hung up.

I booked a rideshare, went back to my hotel, and raided the minibar until I passed out.

52

mackenzie

I woke up Saturday morning with my head pounding. I don't usually drink that much, but last night... last night was different. Bourbon, rum, vodka — whatever was in the minibar that could drown out the noise in my head. If I got drunk enough, maybe the ache in my chest would disappear too.

It didn't.

The light from the bedside lamp pierced through my eyelids as I reached for my phone. I'd turned it off last night. Now it blinked with messages from Alex, David, Grace, Ree — even Evan.

Even Alex.

I didn't respond to any of them, and I was glad I didn't. I could get reckless when I was drunk. After the way I stormed out yesterday, I might already be friendless anyway.

I'd spent the night curled in a dream of Evan's arms. I could still feel him — the warmth, the weight, the way his hand slid across my hip in that easy, familiar way. When I rolled over to the other side of the bed and reached for him, the cold sheets felt like a slap.

Not numb enough.

I forced myself up and into the bathroom. I sat in the tub long after the water went cold. It felt easier to stay there than to get out and face the day. Maybe if I stayed long enough, everyone would forget I existed.

Unfortunately, there was a boat waiting — and David, and Alex. And Evan. I couldn't avoid them forever, even if I wasn't sure I could handle seeing him again.

Last night was my fault. The fight. The way I walked away. The way I always walked away.

What if Evan didn't want to hear another apology? What if I wasn't worth the drama?

But I couldn't help it — I wanted more time. Just one more hour with him. One more moment to feel like maybe this could still be something.

And deep under all of that?

I was angry. With myself.

Why was I like this?

Why did I keep convincing myself I was broken?

I let my brother — my mother, my grandmother — make me believe that I was the problem. That living at all was selfish. I spent thousands of dollars and a decade in therapy trying to fix it. Trying to believe I could be happy.

But every time things got hard — really hard — I fell back into old patterns. I pulled away. I made it proof.

Proof that I didn't deserve this.

I used Alex as my excuse. Said I was doing it for him. Said he was the reason I didn't date seriously.

But I knew better.

When love finally came knocking again, I panicked. One setback and I threw everything away.

I could walk away again. Like I did fifteen years ago.

But that left me with years of quiet — years of wondering.

I didn't want to wonder anymore.

I wanted this life.

My best life included Evan.

But I couldn't stay holed up forever. David had rented a yacht for Alex's acceptance celebration. Of course he had. That man couldn't just clap and say congrats like a normal person.

I had to go. Maybe I could wear sunglasses and keep my mouth shut the entire time.

Right then, someone knocked on the door.

I groaned. "Who is it?"

"David. Open up."

Of course. I cracked the door. "What?"

"I'm not even gonna call you guapa today. You look like death. You taken anything for that hangover yet?" He pushed past me and came in.

"No. I haven't. I just want to be alone. I'll be social on the boat — just not right now."

"I'm not here to be social." He collapsed onto the couch. "I swear I don't understand you. You're cutting off your nose to spite your face. That's the phrase, right?"

I sat next to him and started crying. "I don't understand me either. I want to stop this spiral, but it's too late. Evan's done. I just have to survive the boat today and avoid him for the rest of my life."

He didn't flinch. "You don't think you deserve to be happy. That's your real issue."

I sniffled, wiping my eyes. "My past has truly fucked me up."

David pulled out his phone and started typing.

"What are you doing? I just confessed my greatest flaw."

"Shhh. Take the phone."

I hesitated, but took it.

"I look a mess," I muttered as I stared at the screen.

And then I completely fell apart.

"Rod? Is that really you?"

Tears streamed down my face. It was my brother.

Rod — who I hadn't spoken to in over twenty years.

After our mom died, Grandma Bitsy took custody of us. I poured myself into school. Rod poured himself into his friends. Eventually, he met Clarice, his now wife, and barely spoke to me. One day, he came home from school alone, and I asked him about class in front of our grandmother.

He recoiled. "MacKenzie. I know you mean well, but I feel uncomfortable around you. Kindly mind your own business."

Grandma jumped in to defend me. He answered. But later that night, he cornered me.

"I need you to back off."

I remember asking, "What did I do?"

He looked away. "I miss our parents. And they're gone because of you. Maybe one day we'll get past it. But right now, I'd rather not be around you."

I told him he needed therapy.

He walked out of the room — and out of my life.

Now, here he was.

"MacKenzie. I can't believe we're talking. It's been a long time."

"Yeah," I breathed. I didn't know what to say. The memories hit like a wave.

"You look good."

"So do you. You still with Clarice?"

"Yep. Three kids now. I hear I've got a nephew who's a swimmer. Maybe I'll meet him someday."

"Maybe."

Rod could tell I was holding back.

"Look — I know I've been an ass. I blamed you for everything. For shit that wasn't your fault. We both lost our parents, but I dumped all of it on you. You were right — I needed therapy. I finally got it in my thirties."

I stared. "Then why didn't you call?"

"I was scared. I figured you hated me for how I treated you. I wouldn't have blamed you."

"I never hated you. But I carried what you said for years. I screwed up so much of my life because I believed it."

He nodded. "I know. I just wanted to say — I'm sorry. It wasn't your fault. You didn't deserve the way I treated you. And maybe one day, I can be the kind of brother you deserve."

I sat there, tears still falling, but something shifted.

When he said It wasn't your fault — it felt like something cracked open inside me.

Like some part of me that had been buried finally breathed.

David walked back in.

I stood and hugged him without saying a word.

He hugged me tighter. "I figured if he said it — the person who blamed you the most — maybe you'd believe it. You still have to believe it for yourself. But now at least you've got a little more room to try. Go shower. You've got a party to attend. And a lot of thinking to do."

After he left, I stared at the wall.

Maybe, for the first time in years, I could finally stop running.

From myself.

From Evan.

From love.

53

evan/mackenzie

After last night, I'd accepted that I couldn't reach Mac. She was stuck in a familiar place — the belief that she didn't deserve good things. That she had to atone for surviving when her parents didn't. I remembered that version of her from when we first met. She'd let herself relax. Let herself be happy. We were happy.

And I let it unravel. She ended it — like happiness was karma she had to pay for.

Grace tried to talk to me last night.

"I'm sorry for encouraging the whole Mac and Evan thing," she said, giving me a hug. "I feel like I set you up for failure."

"It's not you. It's her. And it kills me, because I know she loves me. She just can't get out of her own way."

"I thought y'all were there," she said, quiet.

"So did I."

She stood and grabbed the bottle of gin from the minibar. "Here. Make yourself a drink or two. You can vent to me until you fall asleep."

I poured a gin and orange juice. "I'd rather be alone with my misery. But thanks."

"You've tried. Maybe it's time to let go. You're a great guy."

I'd already taken a long swig of the drink by the time she finished. "Thanks. But not great enough." I picked up my phone.

"Don't call her."

"She's not answering. I know her — I just want to leave a pissy voicemail and hang up. I promise."

Grace shook her head and left me to it.

I called her. Twice. Left two messages I don't remember.

Thankfully, I passed out before I could get fully drunk.

This morning, I had a dozen missed messages from my mom and sister asking what the hell happened. I didn't have any answers.

And now there was this yacht party — a celebration I'd looked forward to all week. I wouldn't be able to avoid her. We'd be trapped together on a boat.

I thought this would be one of the best days of my life.

Now, I wasn't ruling out diving off the side and swimming back to shore.

MacKenzie

We'd been on the yacht for a while. I stepped out onto the deck, still stunned that David rented a 70-foot yacht and hired chefs just to celebrate our son's acceptance into the Academy.

The water was peaceful. The sun was warm. The sky was perfect.

And I was miserable.

I'd kept my distance from Evan. From Ree. From everyone, really.

"Hey Mom!"

Alex trotted out behind me.

"Hey, baby. You having fun?" I asked, not looking directly at him. "It's a great boat, huh?"

He joined me at the railing. "Can I ask you something?"

"Of course. You can always talk to me."

He hesitated. "I know you think I'm too young to get it, but I noticed you and Dr. Evan hanging out. Are y'all getting back together?"

I frowned, keeping my eyes on the water. "That's... up in the air." I turned to him. "How would you feel about that?"

He looked confused. "Why does it matter how I feel? It's your life."

"But it would affect you."

"Not really. I mean, I've met Dad's girlfriends. You don't date. Don't you get lonely?"

"I'm fine." I hesitated, then stammered, "Y-y-you don't need to worry about me."

"But I do worry about you. You're my mom. I want you to be happy."

"If you're okay, I'm happy."

He turned toward me, more serious now. "That's not fair. You can't put that on me. One day, I'm gonna leave. College, Olympics — whatever. I don't want you sitting at home alone."

"Has your father been talking to you about this?"

"No. But Gabe and I were wondering what it would be like if we were brothers."

I blinked. "If Evan and I got together?"

He smiled. "Yeah. That'd be dope."

There's that word again.

I leaned down and kissed his forehead. "Thank you, baby. I appreciate you looking out for me. I'll be fine."

"I know you'll be fine, Mom. But I want you to be happy too."

He kissed my cheek and went back inside.

That conversation knocked the wind out of me. I was using Alex as an excuse for playing it safe — but he didn't want that job.

I needed to get away.

I wandered to the upper deck, trying to find a quiet place to fall apart. I wasn't dressed for escape — wedge heels and linen pants — but I didn't care.

I slipped off my shoes and stepped onto the netted trampoline lounge. The waves stretched below me. I sat, legs folded, watching the water ripple beneath the mesh.

I was ridiculous. I had ruined something good. I didn't know if I could ever fix it.

"Damn."

I looked up. Evan stood at the edge of the netting.

"I guess we had the same idea," I said, sarcastic. "Hide on the edge of the world."

He hesitated, then sat — far from me. That stung.

"Let's just sit here in silence," he said, eyes on the horizon. "I don't trust myself to talk to you yet."

But I needed to tell him.

"I'm sorry to break the quiet, but... something happened this morning."

He sighed. "Do I want to know?"

"I think so." I paused. "David found my brother. I talked to Rod today."

Evan turned to me, surprised. "That's... wow. Was it good?"

I nodded, wiping my eyes. "He said it wasn't my fault. That he doesn't blame me anymore. He got therapy too."

Evan raised an eyebrow. "How'd that make you feel?"

"Lighter. Like maybe... I can finally move forward."

He stood. "I hope you do. I wish you the best, Mac."

He took a step back, looking ready to leave. "I can't pretend nothing happened. I was ready to build something with you. I've waited years. We were right there—" He held up his fingers, nearly touching. "And you backed off again. I can't do this again."

He started to leave.

"Wait!" I scrambled to stand, and everything tilted.

He lost his balance, catching the railing just in time.

"Careful!" he warned.

But I kept moving. I needed to talk to him. To fix this.

Of course, I tripped on one of the damn ties — just as the yacht rocked.

He reached for me.

And we both went flying into the ocean.

We surfaced around the same time.

"Mac! Mac!"

"I'm right here!" I treaded water, winded. "And, uh... we're being left behind."

The yacht kept going — for another two or three minutes — before it stopped.

People started yelling from the railing. David. Alex. Gabe. Someone had seen us fall.

Evan swam closer, eyes glinting. "You realize we've done this before."

"At least I can swim now. Thanks to you."

"Well, while we're floating, wanna tell me what was so important that you had to launch yourself into the sea?"

"I'm sorry," I said, voice cracking. "For all of it. For running. For the drama. For being scared. I'm sorry I hurt you."

He looked at me, heart in his eyes but still guarded. "What does that mean, Mac?"

"No games. I don't want to lose you."

I pushed my braids off my face, tears mixing with seawater.

Evan swam closer. Reached out.

"I don't want to lose you either," he said softly, cupping my face.

And then he kissed me — wet, sun-drenched, salty and real.

The boat circled back behind us. But for a few seconds, we floated in our own world.

Together.

54

evan

The captain backed the yacht up, and the crew threw out two buoys to pull us back onto the boat. By then, everyone was standing around, watching us in a mix of awe and laughter.

"Did you push her off?" Liza asked, cocking her head at her brother.

He smiled. "No — actually, she pushed me."

The crew wanted to make sure we were okay, so we got dragged down to one of the bedrooms for a quick evaluation. Once everyone hovered and pushed food at us long enough, we finally managed to get a few minutes alone.

I was nervous. She didn't seem mad. Hell, she didn't even seem shaken. Just... open.

"Okay. You didn't finish what you were saying — before you pushed me into the ocean again," I said, laughing. "Seems to be your way of getting my attention. So, what else are you trying to tell me?"

She looked at me with tears in her eyes — again. We'd been through every emotion in the book these past two days. This week had been a rollercoaster from start to finish — shock, anger, comfort, fireworks, and now this moment. I could see it in her face. She still loved me. Fiercely. Maybe as much as she did 18 years ago.

She let it all out. The conversation with her brother had cracked her wide open, and for the first time, she didn't hold back. She told me everything. Breathlessly. In a hurry. Like she was afraid she'd lose her nerve.

"Was that so hard to say?" I teased, though my voice was softer than before. "Do we have to almost drown before you admit your feelings?"

I pulled her to me and kissed her. Fiercely this time. Then kissed her hand.

"We're different now — but in all the right ways. We've grown. We fell in love as kids. I was this idealistic, one-track-minded guy who only thought about his dreams. But then I met you, and I learned I could chase goals and open my heart at the same time. You didn't even have to try. Just... being you."

She shook her head. "But I'm not the same person I was back then."

"I don't agree. Yeah, when I met you, you were introverted and shy — but I always saw flashes of the woman you'd become. In med school, those glimpses came more often. Now? Now you're a grown-ass woman. Strong. Fully realized. You've been through it and came out the other side. Maybe not totally healed — but who is? You just have to let yourself be happy."

"You were so mad at me last night."

"I panicked. I was tired of holding on just for you to keep running. You acted like my feelings didn't matter. And honestly, I was prepared to accept whatever version of a relationship you offered."

She let out a long, frustrated exhale. "I hope you don't panic like that while you're elbow-deep in someone's brain," she grumbled. "I've been torn for the past four days — blissfully enjoying every moment with you, but knowing there was a deadline hanging over us. Wondering if I could really be happy. And too afraid to try."

"I fucked up. I was scared you were walking away again. But I just needed one night. I would've haunted your ass when we both ended up in Miami with our kids."

She raised an eyebrow at me, lips pursed. "What are we saying, Evan?"

I smiled. "Are we both going to use our words here? Or do you need to throw me back in the ocean?"

She plopped down cross-legged and gave me the same Price Is Right hand motion she used when we first met. "Proceed."

"I love you. That's what it comes down to. But it's not just that. I love you in your quiet moments, your loud moments, your sexy moments, and your stubborn-ass moments. Every version of you has my heart. Even when we weren't in each other's lives — I never stopped loving you. Samantha MacKenzie Stephens, I want to spend the rest of my life basking in your sunshine."

"The sunshine I barely have?"

"Oh, you're sunny enough for me. I don't need another me — I need you."

She jumped up, arms flung around my neck before I could say another word.

"I love you. Just so you're clear. I think I loved you the moment we met. And I love that you've been so damn patient with me. I know I should've handled the San Francisco situation differently — but it's done. I won't be perfect moving forward. I've been taking care of myself — for a long time — but I promise to give you grace if you give me the same."

I kissed her before she could spiral again. A real one. One that said more than words ever could.

When I pulled back, I didn't let her go. I couldn't.

"I'm not letting you go again. Get used to me — wherever we end up."

She grinned. "So... we're moving to Miami? And I'm gonna have a stepson?"

"Quick, fast, and in a hurry. We lost 15 years — but we've got nothing but time now."

She kissed me again and nodded. "So much to do. Sell my house in Nashville. Sell yours in San Fran. Get our licenses transferred, find new practices —"

I kissed her mid-sentence and spun her around.

"We've got time. We'll spend the next month figuring it all out — together."

"Together."

Epilogue

Los Angeles: Nine Weeks Later

Evan

I was on the phone with the contractor for the house in Miami when Gabe came into the room, clearly annoyed.

"Can you help me with the slideshow setup outside? The screen's black but I hear sound."

I held up a hand, finishing the call. "Isn't your mother supposed to be helping with that?"

Gabe groaned. "Dad. Be serious. You know Mom isn't a tech person. I wish Alex was already here — he'd have this figured out in five seconds. You old folks are hopeless."

I adjusted his tie, smirking. "Let me wrap this up. Then I'll see what y'all broke."

Grace peeked her head in. "Crisis averted. There's video now." She motioned Gabe out the room with a shooing gesture.

Gabe made a face, then bolted. Grace turned to me. "How are you feeling? Ready?"

"I've never been more ready for anything in my life."

MacKenzie

"How do I look, Alex? David?" I did a slow twirl after stepping out of the car.

Alex rolled his eyes. "You look great — again. But you know that already. Stop pretending you're not nervous." He kissed my cheek and ran up the steps to Evan's family home.

David grinned. "You look incredible. But the real question is — are you ready?"

"I can't even describe how happy I am."

David tilted his head. "I've never seen you like this. It suits you." He glanced around. "Is everyone here?"

"Plenty of people. It's packed." I pointed toward the overwhelmed valet staff.

David gently tipped my chin. "I'm proud of you. Watching you walk into your happy ending... it gives me hope for mine."

I touched his face, smiling. "I can't wait to meet the woman who finally takes you off the market."

He laughed, but his eyes got misty. "Guapa, solo se feliz — you deserve it."

"Damn it, David, now I'm crying!" I fanned my face, trying to preserve my makeup.

"No tears! Let's get you inside." He held out his hand, and I took it — walking toward the rest of my life.

The Bon Voyage party had officially become a full-blown event. Evan's family showed up in full force — his mother and grandmother, Liza with Eliana, Joe and his wife Trinity, and a few colleagues from the university. Ree was there, along with med school friends and neighborhood families.

A few of my colleagues from Nashville flew out. My brother couldn't make it, which was probably for the best. But we'd spoken since that phone call — even scheduled a joint therapy session once things settled.

The food was unreal. I didn't plan any of it, thank God, but it was catered and over the top. Grazing tables everywhere — vegan, lactose-free, gluten-free, fried Oreos (thank you, Gabe and Alex). Ice cream flown in from Azúcar. An open bar. A string quartet and a DJ. Flowers everywhere. It was more formal than I expected — but somehow, just right.

I slipped upstairs to the guest room to breathe for a minute.

We were really doing this — moving to Miami.

It had been nine weeks since swim camp. The boys were starting their Academy prep in September, and the time between had been a whirlwind.

We found a house in Miami. I sold my house in Nashville — it went fast. Evan's San Francisco home went under contract last week.

The Miami house needed renovations, which we managed remotely. Never again.

Evan had his Florida medical license already, and he'd accepted a job at a neurosurgery department. I was finishing my paperwork and planned to join a pediatric practice part-time — maybe open my own eventually. There was no rush.

For the first time in a long time, there was time.

Evan

I came back downstairs after finishing with the contractor. Renovating from across the country? Never again.

I hugged my mom, grandma, sister — even my ex-wife.

"How's everyone doing?"

Mom poked my shoulder. "Can't believe you're really leaving California."

"For a year," I said. "And we've got space if you want to come visit — or stay."

She raised a brow. "Liza told me Stephon might be transferred too. Somewhere in Florida."

Grace chimed in, "If Gabe stays at the Academy, I'm moving down too. Condo life. I already started looking."

Miss Lorraine added, "If I move, I'd need to sell the house..."

"We'll help with that when it's time," Liza said, stepping in. "Let's just enjoy today."

The DJ's voice boomed through the speakers, calling everyone inside for the slideshow. Gabe looked smug as he led everyone in — proud that he got it to work.

The slideshow started with our family — even old photos of my dad. My mother's breath hitched, but she stayed composed.

Then the tone shifted.

Photos of me and MacKenzie in med school filled the screen. David's voice narrated our love story — how it started, how it ended, and how it had come full circle in the ocean behind a yacht. The crowd erupted in laughter.

Then the quartet began to play *Ave Maria*.

I kissed my family and quietly slipped away.

The DJ ushered everyone to the backyard. The chairs were set. The string quartet paused — then started *At Last* by Etta James.

I walked to the altar with Gabe at my side.

MacKenzie and Alex crossed the lawn toward me. She wore a white satin dress with a halter neckline and heels that glinted under the lights.

She was breathtaking.

My grandmother gasped. "It's a surprise wedding!"

Laughter followed. And just like that — it was happening.

MacKenzie

The ceremony felt like a dream.

If they hadn't filmed it, I don't know how much I'd remember beyond Evan's face.

The look in his eyes. The softness. The knowing.

Alex walked me down the aisle in the dress that fit who I was now — not the girl I had been 15 years ago.

The scent of my bouquet — calla lilies, ferns, petunias.

The vows. The tears. The kiss. The way Evan held me like we were the only two people on Earth.

Our first dance to *Outstanding* — Evan singing softly in my ear.

Every second felt surreal.

Even my brother made it — FaceTimed in for the ceremony.

I'd joke about forgetting Alex in all the magic, but the truth is — he was growing up. And I saw that.

The reception turned into a full dance party. Most of our guests were in their 40s and 50s — so it was all 80s and 90s music. At least we had the good sense not to mosh. One wrong move and somebody's hip would be done.

There was this subtle finality hanging in the air. The end of an era. The end of uncertainty.

Evan was right — it really wasn't too late.

I dragged Grace to the bouquet toss. Ree came, too, though she protested. There were way more single women over 40 than I expected — a fact I mentally bookmarked.

Grace caught it, of course. I hugged her tight. Somehow, she'd become one of my closest friends. Go figure.

And when Evan and I walked out of that backyard hand-in-hand — bubbles flying around us, everyone cheering — I kept thinking about something he'd said during our vows:

My love for MacKenzie was there whether she was near or far, grumpy or happy, anxious or calm, furious or melting into my arms. Our meeting was destiny. Our reconnection was prologue. All versions of her have always had my heart.

Always had. Always will.

We climbed into the back of the limo — heading to the hotel before our abbreviated honeymoon in Key West.

Evan poured champagne into two flutes and handed me one.

I curled up beside him, humming *Outstanding*.

"Sing that to me forever?" he asked, kissing my forehead.

I took a sip and stretched my legs across his lap. "Forever."

"My mom said that was the most beautiful ceremony she's ever seen." He pulled me closer.

I smiled and repeated part of my vows. "Who would've thought the girl afraid of water and her own shadow would end up with a swimming neurosurgeon? Because of you, I can dive into anything now. Including water. Including life. Forever. Ever thine. Ever mine. Ever ours."

"Where did that last part come from?"

"Beethoven. Saw it in a show, looked it up."

Evan's hand slid under my dress. "Didn't know you knew anything about Beethoven."

"He composed great music. I know that much. And he loved his wife."

"And now we've got that in common," he said, kissing my neck.

I giggled as he closed the partition. "Is that so?"

"For the rest of our lives." He kissed me again.

"For the rest of our lives."

About D.W. Brooks

Author, Physician, Kidney Transplant Survivor

I have always been an enthusiastic reader. Breakfast in my childhood home was a slow process, as I would read any object on the table—newspapers, cereal boxes, milk cartons, anything with inscriptions. Taking away my books was an effective punishment.

As part of this interest, my cousins and I created a neighborhood of preteen and teenage characters who had adventures and solved mysteries. We drew out this neighborhood, identified where everyone lived, and created character profiles for each one. We were well ahead of our time and wrote many unfinished stories, which ended up in the attic as we got older. After this failed experiment, I still nurtured thoughts of writing my own stories one day.

Becoming an author was an early dream pushed aside by practical thoughts and fears. Hence, I decided to take a more surefire route of going to medical school and residency. While I didn't write my own stories, I spent time writing in a medical and educational capacity.

A health crisis awakened the desire to write again. And with the ability to self-publish, I could see a path to getting my words and stories out of my head and into a bound book others could read and hopefully enjoy.

The author lives in Texas with her husband and children. She enjoys trying
stay in shape, sporadically cooking, reading (still), writing, and working on
blog. She is eternally grateful to the woman who donated a kidney to her ove
years ago and continues to advocate for organ donation as much as she can.

To learn more about D. W. Brooks and future publications and events, vi
https://authordwbrooks.com